This story is for those who take a chance on love

no matter how slim.....

Dedicated to The Aunt and The Uncle

and Him.

A note to my readers:

I must beg your indulgence and your
patience. To fulfill the terms of my promise,
I had to write this book without using any
names. It's not as confusing as it may
sound. And I always keep my promises.

Chapter One

I was staying with my aunt and uncle that summer watching their children so my aunt, a nurse, could care for my ill grandmother. My aunt came home one day and invited me to go camping with her family up on the St. Lawrence River. I was feeling lonely, so I agreed to go along. I had never been camping before and my birthday was a few days away. I decided to give myself a little present and started to pack.

The children sensed the excitement that had infected the house because they were very hard to control the next day. Being three- and one-year-old at the time, they were very rambunctious. But on the day we left, they were impossible. I decided the best thing to do was put my things in the camper and keep the children busy so my aunt and uncle could pack the rest without interruption.

The ride to the state park was uneventful. Except for a few breaks for my cousins and snacks for the adults, the hours flew by. We arrived at the campground early so we had to wait for the campsite to be ready. I ran around, literally, keeping the children busy and getting to know the two families who had come up with us in our 'camper convoy'.

My uncle's friends had a son just a little younger than myself and the two planned to spend as much time on the river fishing as they possibly could. My aunt and her friend were reminiscing about events that had happened during previous camping trips.

After the sites were ready, the men settled the campers and the women walked behind them, still trying to stretch our legs after the long ride. As with packing, I decided the best thing to do was keep the children busy so my aunt and uncle could balance, hook up the water and electric, and unpack the camper. I was glad I had during supper that evening. My aunt thanked me and explained it was so much easier with both eyes on her work, instead of one on that and one on the kids.

She also told me that their friends' granddaughter was spending a few days with her grandparents; I would have someone to talk to. It seemed like a good idea to me at the time, but I had no idea what havoc we would make of my life.

As it turned out, our friends at home were our neighbors at the campground. When the granddaughter arrived, we waited a respectable amount of time for their family to have a few private moments, and then walked over. I was introduced to the granddaughter and we became fast friends. We talked about school and boys. We were both teenagers, so one could assume that the subject would turn towards the opposite sex sooner or later.

We all went to bed that night happy and exhausted. I thought, 'If the rest of the vacation turned out this nice, it wasn't a wasted trip'.

The next day started as uneventful as all the others had. This, I learned later, was the calm before the storm. My uncle had seen a man riding a jet-ski earlier that afternoon and wanted to watch him take it out of the water and ask him a few questions about it. My aunt decided to go with him. Since I had never seen or even heard of a jet-ski, I told them I would wait for my younger cousin to wake up from his nap. Then, I would bring him down to the boat launch so I could see this thing, too.

My cousin slept longer than usual that day. By the time we reached the launch, the man and machine had vanished; and so had my aunt and uncle. We walked, or rather I walked and carried my cousin, back to the camper. I met the granddaughter, my new friend, there and we decided to take a walk later that night and leave the adults to themselves.

Looking back on that night, I can't honestly say whether I should have stayed at the camper and toasted marshmallows with the rest of the extended family or taken that walk. I'm glad I did, though. That walk started the most wonderful experience of my life. I wouldn't change what happened for fifty-million dollars.

We were simply wandering around in circles, talking and generally having fun, free from the adults. I was making her laugh with my phony accents. I could do French, German, Swedish, English, Scottish, and Southern Belle accents. We happen to be walking by this one particular campsite with an ordinary gray dome tent and a fire going in the little brick fireplace on the roadside of the site. The object that caught my attention, though, was the jet-ski on the back of a truck.

It wasn't really the jet-ski that caught my eye, but the man tying it down. I couldn't see well through the dark, but I saw he was tall with dark hair. I watched him and noticed how well-built he was. I didn't know how well until he came around the side of the truck into full view. He had broad shoulders and muscular build. He was wearing shorts and his legs were long and trim. He took the few steps to the picnic table with easy, confident strides. I knew he was something to look at and I now had to know more. Before I realized what I was doing, I swerved off the path we were walking and started straight for him.

I had been talking with a German accent and thought it would be fun to see his face if I spoke to him that way. I hesitated until I saw I had his attention, then walked up to him and asked, "Ish dat schor get-ski?"

He looked at me very surprised and said, "Why, yes. It is. Would you like to see it?" I motioned to my friend and we all walked to the back of the truck.

He said hello to my friend and I introduced her, then he started in talking about the jet-ski. He seemed so relaxed, leaning his elbow on his truck and pointing out a few things. Sure, everyday strange girls walk into his campsite and start talking to him, right? I realized I had wandered too far away in my thoughts because the next thing I remember, he was asking my friend where she was from.

He turned to ask me a question and suddenly realized that he didn't even know my name. My friend introduced me as a foreign exchange student from Germany! You could have knocked me over with a feather. I didn't figure there was any harm in it. The chances we were ever going to see him again were slim. We visited for a while and, after the usual small talk, we all knew each other's ages and most of our school histories. My age was completely false, though. Nervously, I noticed the time. I had an eleven o'clock curfew, so we left and walked back to our perspective campsites.

My uncle and his fishing buddy were still out at the picnic tables joking around. When we told them what happened, they couldn't stop laughing. It seemed perfectly harmless at the time. I told my aunt about it when I went into the camper to go to bed. She didn't think it was such a good idea, but, of course, I didn't listen.

The next morning I couldn't stop talking about him to my aunt. She asked me how old he was. When I revealed that he was twenty-four, she had a strange look on her face. I had just turned sixteen earlier in the week. I'm not sure if it was surprise or concern on her face. She told me she knew me well enough to know that I liked him and wanted to see him again.

She told me if it looked like he returned the feeling, it would be best to be honest with him before a 'real' relationship started. When she said that, the sinking feeling in my stomach began. I didn't know how I was going to make it happen, but I had to see him again. I knew he worked nearby. I assumed he would be back around five o'clock.

My friend and I were out walking again, before supper this time, and we saw him out riding the jet-ski on the river. I casually sauntered to the end of the dock to watch him. If I wanted him to notice me noticing him, that was the perfect spot.

He had been on his way in when I walked out, and, when he saw us, started back out and proceeded to show off. He would hit waves and jump them, then run in figure-eights, splashing water everywhere.

We watched for some time then started to walk back to the shore. I gave up trying to be noticed had started to think he was still out on the water waiting for us to walk away, to avoid us. But when he noticed us leaving, he started in. We stopped and waited for him to load the jet-ski onto the truck and began chatting.

I have to say, he looked even better in the light of day than by the firelight of the night before. His hair wasn't as dark as it had appeared and, being wet, was tossed around by the wind coming from the river. He had a strong, square chin that could set tight with stubbornness or soften when he laughed. He had large hands that weren't afraid of hard work, but could also hold you tight or gently brush away a tear.

He reached in his truck and grabbed his glasses, then bent to tie his shoes. That's when I noticed his eyes. He looked up when I spoke and his eyes were the most stunning color. They weren't quite blue but not really green. I knew right then I had to get to know him better so I could recognize the emotions I saw flashing in those depths.

I have always believed one could read another's mind by reading the looks in their eyes. One could see pain, happiness, anger, fear, or love. Love I wasn't sure I could recognize, though. I had never seen it except in the eyes of my family.

Now why was I thinking such a thing? I thought about what I was wearing, shorts and a t-shirt. When I was told we were going camping, I packed camp clothes. I hadn't even bothered packing my makeup or even a simple pair of earrings. A man this handsome and mature could find nothing attractive in a girl like me. It was a preposterous thought. Then why was he looking at me like that?

He asked what we were doing later that night. When we said nothing, he stood straight and suggested, "Why don't you come over? It gets pretty lonely out here at night."

We said we would and watched him get into his truck and drive away.

I was so excited about the invitation that I could hardly eat supper. I told my aunt we were going for another walk later.

"If you're going to see that guy again, why don't you just say so?" she laughed.

I assured her there was nothing to worry about; my friend would be there the whole time. She nodded that she wasn't worried, but just remember my curfew.

I helped clear away the dishes, changed into the nicest clothes I could with my limited wardrobe, then sat around trying not to seem over anxious. Finally, my uncle had had enough of my pacing and told me if I was going, to go once. He laughed as I fairly ran over to the other campsite and grabbed my friend. I heard him make a wise crack about teenagers as I left, but I paid no attention.

The first time we walked by; he wasn't there. I don't know how I managed to walk around the park with my heart in my feet. But the second time we walked by, he had returned. He was sitting at the picnic table, watching us walk towards him. I wish I knew what he was thinking as that smile began to creep from his face into his eyes.

There were no formalities this time. We were all talking like old friends, sitting across the table from each other, and having a good time. Though, I was melting inside. He was talking to my friend, but looking directly at me. I took a chance and winked at him just to see what he would do. He winked right back.

My friend noticed this and excused herself. I was torn as to whether I wanted her to leave or not, but I'm glad she did. I think I heard her say, "I think it's time I went and left you two alone," and she was gone. He and I barely noticed her leave, absorbed in staring at each other.

I was suddenly scared to be alone with him and I fearfully suggested, "Maybe I had better go, too. It's getting late."

He grabbed my hand when I tried to get up from the picnic table. "Don't go. Stay a little longer and talk. All I would do is go to bed anyways, and this is more fun than sleeping on the ground," he said and half laughed simultaneously nervous and hopeful.

I said, "All right," and sat back down. He didn't let go of my hand. He comfortably held it in both of his in his lap and kept talking as if nothing at all was different. I don't remember what he was saying as I was still trying to recover from the electric shock that had gone through me when he touched my hand.

I had to concentrate on what I was saying before I answered his questions. I was still playing the part of the exchange student and had to make sure my accent was correct before I spoke a word.

It would have been so easy to tell him the truth. But things were just beginning and I didn't want to ruin them before they could go further. The thought crossed my mind that I quite possibly could be ruining things by keeping up this charade, but I pushed it far back in my mind, along with the growing knot in my stomach.   I didn't want to think about anything except the sensations running through me from his fingers.

He was studying my hand, turning it this way and that, and rubbing his thumb over the fingers absently while he talked. Then he did something incredible, amazing, romantic, or shocking, depending on your own state of mind. He stopped, mid-sentence and held our hands together, comparing them.

"You have very small hands. Did you know that?" He brought it up to his mouth and kissed it. Shivers still run up my spine when I think of it.

"Very soft. Is the other one just as soft as this one?" he asked as he reached for my other hand. "Yup, it is," he said.

We sat there for ages, facing one another across the picnic table bench, each studying the other's face, with both my hands in each of his.

"Well, my fire is going out," he said and jumped up to put some wood on the fire. I wasn't sure what to do, so I turned and watched him kneeling by the fire.

He saw me staring into the fire and said, "It's pretty mesmerizing, isn't it?"

I was surprised to hear him talk about that way a fire. He had a sensitive side, I realized. Somehow his rough exterior didn't match his heart. That intrigued me.

'There I go again,' I berated myself, 'heart means love. For Pete's sake, you just met the man!'

To lighten the mood, I decided to carry my prank a little further and asked, "Mesmerizing?"

My efforts were wasted though. He looked at me and I was lost in his eyes as the fire reflected off them.

"Hypnotic, almost. You know," he said as he crossed in front of me to sit at my side. "You can stare at it for hours and your mind just kind of goes blank, but it has fifty-million things running through it all at the same time."

For as long as I live I will never forget that explanation. He had put his finger precisely on the definition. I knew at that moment this was one special man and I was falling hard and fast for him.

He reached over and turned me towards him, "Understand?"

"Yes, I understand," I answered in a whisper. My impulsiveness took over and I leaned forward and kissed him.

I'm not sure if it could be classified as a kiss. It was more like a whisper or the soft brush of an artist's pen across his paper; picture perfect.

I leaned back far enough to read the reaction on his face. His eyes were closed, and when he opened them, a lazy smile spread across his lips.

"I was beginning to get scared that you wouldn't do that," he breathed, happily laughing.

"Scared of a kiss?" I asked, disbelieving.

He leaned forward and stopped just inches from me. "American Humor," he said against my lips.

He finished what I had started earlier, but his kiss was no whisper. His lips moved over mine in an ancient rhythm as timeless as the river itself. His mouth parted and his tongue slid across my lips. It didn't prod or try to bully its way through, but sweetly beckoned to my own. I started to answer its call when we heard a camper door slam.

We pulled apart, but when I tried to pull further away, his arm tightened to keep me close to him. Out of nervousness of not knowing what to do next, I looked at my watch and saw it was twenty minutes to eleven.

I guiltily jumped up and reminded him of my curfew. He said smiling it was all right, that if I have to go, I have to go. I took one or two steps backwards when he stood up and took my face between his hands.

"How do you say 'good night' in your language?" he asked.

I told him the few words I knew for the phrase and he repeated each after me.

"Good night," he whispered, and kissed me one last time.

I walked back to my aunt and uncle's camper with my heart pounding so hard I was out of breath when I reached it. They were both still out at the picnic table, but I didn't feel up to talking. I wanted to be alone to relive the evening over and over in my mind.

As I was changing for bed, I pulled my shirt over my head and noticed it still had the smell of his cologne on it. I climbed under the covers and held it close to me as I fell asleep.

Chapter Two

The next morning I was surprised to find myself full of energy, though I hadn't slept a wink the night before. I had the strangest dreams. Not dreams exactly, more like memories. His touch was like the fire he was staring into. His eyes drifting in and out of emotions like the river swelling past. Memories of the evening's sensations crept in through my subconscious and, after each one, I woke up and had to fall asleep again. Needless to say, it wasn't a rest full sleep.

I helped with breakfast and even fixed my aunt's hair. We had plans to go to a zoo in Canada and the children were excited about seeing the animals. I simply wanted to keep busy during the day so it would seem that the night came that much faster.

As the day wore on, the apprehension I was beginning to feel turned from a slight gnawing sensation to one more excruciating. I was beginning to doubt he would want to see me. I was beginning to think I didn't want to see him. I was beginning to, well, doubt everything and anything. I had never been known for self-control and my impulses had possibly gotten me in over my head this time.

'Not possibly… most probably,' I told myself. I thought I would wait a while and see what would happen if I left things to themselves. I adopted a 'whatever is going to happen will happen' attitude.

The zoo was fun. The raccoons were hilarious! We bought popcorn to feed them and they fell all over themselves trying to grab it as we threw it in their cage. It's odd, in a way, a zoo full of animals, and the only one's I remember are the 'coons. Someday I would like to go back and see what I missed.

Back at the campground, supper was a solemn affair. The children were cranky because they had missed their nap and their mood spread throughout all three adults at the table. I was very relieved when they fell asleep immediately after the meal. We cleaned up the dishes and went over to our neighbor's campsite where a fire was already blazing even though the sun hadn't gone down yet.

My friend suggested that we go for a walk. Again, away from everyone else we could be silly and fun and free together. However, everyone else thought that was a great idea also and decided to go for ice-cream at the small store near the beach.

I did not want to go. I had been stung by a wasp the last time we had gone up. They are attracted to the sticky candy wrappers in the garbage cans. I sat down on a bench near one of the cans. I decided to sit back and cross my legs to enjoy myself and never saw the wasp on my leg. When it saw that it was trapped and couldn't fly away, it let me have it. I couldn't straighten my leg fully for nearly two days after. Needless to say, I avoided that store for the rest of the trip and never went near it when we went to the beach.

Tonight was different. I thought I could walk casually by his tent and get a feel of the atmosphere there. My aunt saw me walking faster than usual and told me to take my time. "If he's worth all this dancing around, don't ruin it by running up to him. Play a little hard to get."

Hard to get: Hook 'em then take your time reeling them in, The only problem with that theory is that guys have known about it for years, and have been doing it themselves. My question is: If two people are both playing the same game, how do you know when the game is over and who wins?

'No, no games. Tonight I tell him the truth and let the chips fall where they may,' I told myself. 'I am a bright, intelligent young woman who obviously has some form of attraction for him to have kissed me last night. Look at how you dressed: shorts, t-shirt, no make up. There is something there. If he really likes me, he'll take a chance and get to know who I really am and not some stupid foreign exchange student!' This little pep talk was all I needed. My mind was made up and my convictions were set.

"I hope," I whispered as we neared his campsite.

His truck was there. He was busy writing something and shuffling papers around in his brief case. He looked up when he heard voices. I waved and he waved back, then immediately went back to what he was writing. It felt like somebody had thrown a bucket of ice water on me.

All of my convictions disappeared with an audible 'poof'. If I left things to themselves, like I had decided only seconds earlier, they would mess themselves all up. I knew a plan was needed.

I grabbed my friend's arm and motioned for her to follow me. We walked over to the building that held the bathrooms and showers. I had noticed earlier that there were boats sailing up and down the river with bright, multi-colored sails. I told her that I was nervous about going over to see him alone and could she please come with me.

"After a while, say something about the boats. If it doesn't look like he wants to see me, I will follow you down to see them. But if he does…" I trailed off, not knowing how to end.

"You want me to excuse myself and leave, right?" she finished for me.

I thanked her for understanding and especially for going along with my hair-brained scheme. We both took a deep breath and walked over to where he was seated.

He looked up as we approached, hesitated a little, then smiled and put down his pen. I tried to read what was in his eyes to see what he was thinking. I couldn't be sure that I was accurately reading what was there, but it looked like he was hiding something.

He started talking to my friend immediately and wouldn't even look at me. I stood there kicking myself for being so stupid. I started to think it was her he really was interested in and was just pretending to like me so she would come around more often. The hard-to-get, jealousy combo game. If that was true, then he was just toying with me the night before. 'You are such a fool!' I berated myself. Here he was, talking to my friend, a beautiful, dark-haired woman a couple years older than me, as if I wasn't anywhere near them.

I snapped back from my thoughts as I heard her mention the boats. "…and I thought I would go down to watch them," she was saying.

"That's a good idea. Maybe we will see you down there later," he said.

He was looking directly at me. I hadn't noticed that he turned on the bench. Instead of his legs being under the table, he had stretched towards the fireplace and leaned back against the table with his elbows resting on the top. All I could think about was how good those arms had felt around me and I wished my friend and him much happiness. Wait a minute, did he say 'we'?

My head snapped up from the ground I had been studying during my reverie and I met his eyes. He was still staring straight at me as my friend walked away to join her family at the store. Again, we never noticed her leave being lost in our own world. All I can say is I was stunned! I had no idea what to do or say. I just stood looking back at him with a dopey look on my face, holding my breath.

He sat up and motioned to the seat next to him. I walked over and sat down. My brain was sending signals to my mouth but my tongue wasn't listening. The only thing I could think to say was, "How was your day at work?"

He looked at me as a lazy smile spread across his face. "It was pretty good. The usual dirt and concrete."

I had a questioning look on my face because he started to explain he tested the backfill that went into the prison they were building nearby.

He put his papers into his brief case and closed the top. I commented how nice it was. Yet again, the only words my mouth would form.

He boasted his sister had given it to him at his college graduation. He pointed out the lock and informed me he could never forget the combination because it was his birthday. I filed that date away with the rest of my important dates for future reference.

I noticed the party had broken up at the store and people were walking past, looking at us strangely. I made a mental check of everything around us that could be considered incriminating: blouse buttoned all the way up; respectable distance between us; no crumbs on either of us from supper. So what were the looks for?

My aunt started walking towards us, and, the closer she got, the harder my heart pounded. 'Please, please,' I prayed and begged her in my mind. 'Don't say anything. I have everything under control.'

She had this strange look on her face, part anger and part concern. I thought that was it, right then and there, it's all over, busted.

I introduced her to him and they exchanged the usual pleasantries. I dropped my eyes guiltily to my feet as they talked and an indescribable feeling of shame washed over me.

I looked up as she said she was leaving and she gave me stern look with a nod in his direction, as if to say, 'TELL HIM!'

I couldn't get over that feeling of shame. I had done something wrong and I knew it. I also knew how to make things right. 'Just do it,' I preached to myself. 'Walk him over to the picnic table, sit him down, and tell him the truth. If he never wants to see you again, you only have yourself to blame.'

After my aunt left, he walked over to put his briefcase in his truck. He turned back to me and, seeing that particular look, all my convictions, once again, gone.

"Would you like to go see the boats?" he asked. He had the most tender look on his face that I couldn't have said no, even if I had wanted to. I nodded yes and we started to walk together towards the river.

I will always look back on that afternoon as the beginning. The way he looked at me made me melt. I know that sounds clichéd, but that is the only word that seems to fit. Every time after that first look only succeeded in endearing him to my heart even more.

We walked to this part of the river bank that was very secluded. The only way to see us was from the river itself or by walking out to the very edge of the dock. The river rolled by and lapped at the rocks jutting out near shore.

The boats were gone. The sun was just setting; so we decided to stay. We didn't say anything. I'm not sure how to describe the mood but to just call it peaceful. A few motor boats were coming in and docking for the night. A few ducks swam past, but there was no other movement.

We didn't touch or even look at each other. We just felt each other's presence. It was enough to know that each *wanted* to be with the other.

Eventually, I turned to say something about the river and saw him studying me. His face had softened and the look in his eyes was of an overpowering emotion I didn't recognize yet. He seemed struggling against something inside. His eyes changed immediately when he noticed I was watching him, also. Things were getting entirely too serious and I had to do something to lighten the mood or I might explode.

I took a step closer to the bank and leaped onto a flat rock sticking out from the water. I looked back to make sure he was watching me and proceeded to jump from rock to rock.

"You're going to fall in," he hollered from the shore. What he didn't know was that I wanted to fall in; not so he could rescue me from the probably cold waters of the river, but so he would laugh again.

'I want to make him laugh,' I thought, as I looked at the slippery rock beneath me, 'not crack my head open.' I started to jump to another rock and lost my balance. I instinctively reached out for anything to hold me onto that rock. I felt his hand grab mine. He pulled me to shore and into his arms.

"What was the purpose of that?" he asked, thoroughly and completely confused.

"I just couldn't stand still anymore," I answered and looked up into his face. "Boy, you have nice eyes," I thought out loud, not realizing I had said anything.

"Oh, come on, that has got to be the oldest line in the book!"

"I'm serious," I said back. "You can tell a lot about a person from their eyes. Yours are the nicest blue-green I have ever seen."

My slip-up and confession were purely impulsive. I only had a heartbeat to regret saying them.

"They're not blue or green." he said, reaching into his back pocket. "See? Here's my license. What does it say right there?"

He was pointing to the abbreviation of eye color on his driver's license where it had typed 'H-A'. I glanced over the card quickly and noted a few things, such as height, home address, and confirmed his birth date. Suddenly, a great idea for a joke hit me.

"HA," I said, and started laughing. "Your license doesn't even agree with you."

"It's not 'ha'. It's h-a. It stands for hazel," he said impatiently, putting his wallet back in his pocket. "And stop laughing, it wasn't that funny!"

"I'm sorry, I couldn't help it," I said, gasping for breath and trying to calm down.

Calming down was to be a futile effort. He took me by my upper arms and kissed me. It was a gentle yet searching kiss; as if he could find the answers he was looking for by punishing my lips with his tenderness. When he felt my arms slide up around his neck, he slid his arms around my waist and deepened the kiss ever so slightly. After what seemed like an eternity, he slowed the kiss with a few last nibbles to my bottom lip.

I sighed quietly to myself, 'nothing is that perfect'. He was looking at me with his revealing eyes. I wanted to crawl inside and shuffle through his thoughts to find the answers to questions of my own.

"What was the purpose of that?" I asked him, repeating his earlier question. He hadn't released his arms from around my waist, only loosened them a little when I spoke. I ran my hands up and down his arms, reveling in the simple sensation of holding each other.

"Well, I had to find some way to make you stop laughing at me," he said and cocked his head at me. He had this habit of leaning his head to one side as he made a joke, I realized. It made him so irresistibly handsome; I just hugged him hard to me.

He turned me around in his arms and we watched the last of the sunset just holding each other, content.

We held hands walking back to his campsite. I sat down at the picnic table and he unloaded some wood from the back of his truck to start a fire. I watched, admiring the way he moved and how easily he threw the chunks of wood around. I had always had a weakness for muscular men, but it wasn't just his looks that had attracted me to him. There was someone underneath his tough exterior, a person I intended to find and get to know.

He came back to the picnic table and sat next to me, putting his arm around me. We talked about his high-school and college careers and my plans for the future, which were many. I wasn't all that careful with what I told him. My answers were honest, but with an accent. He still had no idea that I wasn't a twenty-one-year-old exchange student, but a sixteen-year-old junior in high school. Or so I thought.

Around 10:45 I reminded him about my curfew, and he offered to walk me home. We had spent the last five hours talking, laughing, kissing, sharing, and the next fifteen minutes seemed too much to waste. We were having the oddest conversation about how we knew things about other people that they didn't know we knew.

"I know something about you," he said suddenly.

"What, that I'm not a virgin?" I asked, jokingly.

"No, that's not it," he said, then grinned, "but that's good to know. OW!" The last he shouted because I had punched him in the arm. We stopped under a street light in the road and he rubbed his arm.

"I was only kidding," he laughed.

"Then I'm sorry," I apologized. "Now what is this big secret you know?"

"You tell me!" he said. There was a pleading note in his voice I couldn't ignore.

'Oh my God!' I cursed. 'He knows. Now how do I tell him without his getting mad at me? I never should have started this. Damn!' I cursed again. I couldn't get my brain to think of anything to say. I should have just blurted out, "You probably know I'm not an exchange student, but I am German," and braced for the explosion.

I couldn't look in his eyes anymore. He was looking at me with breathless expectation, and what I thought was hope. I couldn't bear to see the hurt my confession would surely bring. I looked down to where he was holding my hand and absently rubbing his thumb over it. I watched his other hand come up under my chin and I closed my eyes as he tilted my head up to his.

"Oh, come on! It's not like you murdered anybody," he said laughingly. I opened my eyes to look into his and saw his laughter hadn't reached them. He changed suddenly and looked at me intensely, as if by catching and holding my eyes he could burn what he had to say into my soul.

"I want you to know, there is nothing in this world you can't tell me. Understand?" I nodded and looked back at our hands, trying hard to swallow the lump in my throat.

"Let's get you home," he said, giving my hand a gentle squeeze.

We shared one lingering kiss good night when we reached my campsite and he asked if he would see me the next day. I told him we weren't leaving until the end of the week. It was a simple answer to what I thought was a simple question.

"You know what I mean," he said, exasperated.

"Yes," I said, standing on tip-toe to give him another kiss. 'If you want to have anything to do with the real thing,' I thought.

In the camper I didn't say much. The past evening, with all its tenderness and kisses and unspoken emotion, swam in front of my eyes. I had to find a way to tell him. What I was to find later, was that somebody already had.

Chapter Three

I woke up the next morning, took a shower, and, on my way back to the camper, I took a look at his campsite and smiled. His truck wasn't there, but his tent was. I figured he had gone to work and thanked God he hadn't left for home. Staring at the picnic table where we had had such a good time, I new the charade had to end, and soon.

During breakfast, my aunt dropped the bomb. I certainly did not expect what I was about to hear, and I did not know what the hell to expect next.

She asked me if I had told him the truth the night before. I said, "My brain thought of the right words, but my mouth just wouldn't say them. He is really special," I paused, smiling and replaying parts of the evening over in my head, "but I don't know how to tell him without him getting mad at me."

"Well, you don't have to now," she said, closing her eyes and taking a deep breath. "That's why I was trying to get your attention. Your friend's grandfather took it upon himself to tell him the truth."

I was absolutely stunned. All I could do was cry, "Why?!"

"I guess your friend was jealous about you 'getting' him and threw a temper tantrum. Her grandfather thought that if he could break you two up, she could step in and get what she wanted. He went up to the store earlier that everybody so he could carry out his plan. He told all of us about it when we were eating our ice-cream. He tried to make it sound like he was doing the guy a favor by telling him the truth, but I know different. By the way, your friend told us about the boat plan. Pretty ingenious; dangerous, but ingenious."

So that was it. The strange looks when everyone walked by the night before; my aunt's eyes filled with anger and concern; and his cold-shoulder treatment when we first walked up to him. Now it all made sense. 'But why did he keep me around? He could have ignored me and I would haven taken the hint,' I questioned myself.

To say I was confused would be a huge understatement. Now what do I do? Tell him what he already knows because he deserves to hear the truth and explanation from me? Why did he keep me around? Why didn't my friend tell me she was interested in him? What was the attraction that made him stay? When did …? Why the heck…? If…? The questions flying around in my mind resembled a chaotic flock of bats darting out from every corner of my thoughts, then, terrified by the light, scrambling back into a hidden recess for safety.

"One other thing," my aunt was saying. "I heard that things were getting pretty hot and heavy over there last night."

"But nothing—"I started to explain.

"Just let me finish," she interrupted and waited for me to calm down. "Your friend came back from another walk she took later and announced she didn't like the way things looked over there. I asked her what she meant and she said that you were sitting on his lap, necking. When I started laughing, she said 'I don't know why you let her keep going over there. I'm the one who should be over there. I'm older! How can you trust the guy? You hardly know him.' I couldn't believe her grandparents were letting her have this hissy-fit. But anyways, I said, 'I don't have to trust him, I trust my niece. And if he can't be trusted, then you shouldn't be over there either.' Well, she didn't like that much and huffed off into their camper." I thought I saw laughter in her eyes, but I couldn't be certain.

"Let me tell you one more thing before you hear it from someone else. When your uncle went to the bathroom last night, I had him look over and see what was going on. He came back and said it looked like you were helping him stoke the fire. I didn't mean to spy on you, and I do trust you, but something your friend said got to me. He is eight years older than you are and I wouldn't want you to get into a situation you couldn't get out of." She reached across the table and patted my hand.

"Just to set the record straight," I said, enjoying the fact that I could be honest and talk to my aunt like a person. "We did kiss and I did sit on his lap. But other than that, he was a perfect gentleman and didn't try a thing. It's not like that. We enjoy just being in each other's company. But if I knew you were watching, I would have spiced it up a little," I finished lightly, needing to relax.

She laughed briefly the looked at me seriously. "So, what are you going to do now?" she asked. She had never seen me like this. This woman had watched me grow up. Every time she saw me, I had grown into a new stage of my life. Now I was sitting across from her a confused woman obviously feeling very strong feelings. In a way, she was as lost about this whole thing as I was.

"To be honest, I have no idea," I answered, shaking my head.

I was being honest. I did not have a clue. I thought I could just stay out of sight, avoid everyone, and hope he went home that night. 'But that would mean never seeing him again,' I argued. I could bite the bullet and march right up to him and explain the whole situation like I should have done days ago. 'But that would mean having to face him and look in his eyes,' I argued again.

I continued debating with myself for the entire morning and the better part of the afternoon. 'I could be a coward and write him a letter,' I suggested to myself. That was it! I had always fancied myself a writer. I could think of what to say and put it down exactly the way I wanted it. My cowardly side won.

I checked the time and knew I would have to hurry. I thought I could finish the letter and tie it to the strings of his tent before he returned.

I grabbed the notebook I always carry with me and started to write:

I know you know I'm not a foreign exchange student by now. I live in a little town about two hours from here and the couple I have been staying with are my aunt and uncle.

Let me explain. I had no intention of tricking you or carrying this so far. I'm sorry if I hurt you. I tried so many times to tell you the truth, but I didn't know how. I thought, if I told you, you would get mad at me and throw me out of your campsite, or even say you never wanted to see me again. Especially that you never wanted to see me again. I don't want that to happen.

I know we haven't known each other long, but I know enough to know that you are really special and I'd like to spend more time with you.

I'm not sure how you feel about that, but I'd like for you to get to know the real me.

Meet me down by the river near the rocks where we watched the boats. I'd like to apologize in person. See you about five o'clock. If you don't show, I'll understand.

I signed it, folded it, and slipped it into the pocket of my shorts. I put my notebook away, told my aunt I was going to the bathroom, and headed for his campsite.

My plan was flawlessly executed—until I rounded the corner of the bath house and saw his truck there. He had returned from work early and was unloading wood from his truck.

'Shit,' I swore under my breath. My mother had never allowed me to swear, but that was the only word that completely vented my frustration. My picture of what was to happen had crumbled into a million pieces and fell to the ground so hard I could hear them crash.

'Well, now you have to face him,' I thought. I braced myself and decided to A) walk boldly up to him, B) hand him the letter, and C) turn and run like a coward.

The first part of the new plan worked perfectly. I walked over slowly until he noticed me coming. He smiled that smile and said hello. I took the next few steps hesitantly.

I was standing in front of his tent and he walked over to it. "I'm going to let this thing dry out a little," he said, pulling out the stakes. It rolled over and hit me in the leg.

"Excuse me," he said. His voice sounded strange, like he was saying, 'What are you, stupid? Can't you even get out of the way if something is going to hit you?'

I was frozen to the spot. I stepped back out of the way before the tent hit me again. I was trying to think of something to say when I gave him the letter, rather than thrusting it in his hands and leaving without a word. Something in the tone of his voice gave me courage. That sounds contradictory, but I said to myself, 'You have made about the biggest fool out of yourself that you possibly could. You have absolutely nothing to lose!'

"I have something for you," I said and held the letter out to him.

"Thank you," he said, took it and partially unfolded it.

"Don't read it now!" I quickly said, knowing that if there was any mystery in what was contained in the letter, it was gone after that comment. He folded it up and laid it on the table.

"Well, I have to be going. I told everyone I was just going to the bathroom." I never gave him a chance to answer. I started backing up and decided to carry out the third part of my plan. I didn't exactly turn and run, but I walked very fast.

Back at the camper, I heard each and every second tick away until five o'clock. My aunt and uncle decided to go fishing together after supper, which meant I would be watching the children. My aunt always asked me if I minded babysitting before she left to go anywhere. I couldn't very well say, "No, you can't go fishing with your husband because I want to meet some guy who may or may not even be there." I wished them luck and, when five o'clock rolled around, I bundled the kids into their stroller and started for 'our' place by the river.

I decided, rather than walking along the road then trying to push the stroller through the trees, I would walk along the river. It looked smooth enough.

I was almost to the designated spot when I saw him. He was leaning against a tree drinking a soda and watching the river. 'Don't get too excited,' I cautioned myself, 'you wanted to apologize in person, maybe he just wants to tell you off in person.' He turned and saw me struggling to push the stroller over the grass and laughed.

"This wasn't my idea," I said, gesturing to the children.

He said, "That's o.k. but we really didn't need a chaperone."

I wasn't sure if that was good or bad, so I asked.

"Well, I'm sure not going to try anything in broad daylight," he laughed. "No accent. I like it," he added quietly. Watching his face soften when he looked at me and the emotions flashing in his eyes, not to mention the simple fact that when he was close to me there was electricity in the air, made me start to feel hopeful.

"I'm so sorry about that. Like I said in the letter, I had no intention of letting it go this far. I was going to tell you last night, but I couldn't. Can you ever forgive me?" I asked sincerely.

"Oh, I think we can manage that," he said, cocking his head. He reached over and set his soda down on a cement lean-to that covered a water pump and crossed the few feet separating us. Reaching over to touch my face, he looked at me tenderly and said, "You know, I don't even know your name."

I told him my full name, all four of them. "Is there a shorter form than that?" he asked, laughing.

I told him my nickname and he smiled, repeating it. All I could do was look back up at him with wonder and allow myself a small sigh of relief. I knew at that moment, everything would be all right.

I noticed my uncle's boat docking and knew I better meet them and help with supper. I told him as much and then asked him hopefully if I could see him later.

"I'll be there," he said, vaguely.

"I know that; but if you don't want to see me, I won't come over."

"You better come over or I'll come and get you." He smiled again and gave me the look that always my heart dance.

I said, "See you later," and turned towards the dock. Before my aunt and uncle and I walked to the camper, I looked back and saw him emerging from the trees. He walked with such ease, not the gangly uncoordinated gait of most tall men. I still wasn't sure what there was about him, like an aura. 'Tonight is going to be a fresh start,' I thought. Supper couldn't go by fast enough.

I told my aunt the day's events during supper that night. I think she approved. She said she was proud of the way I handled the situation. Maybe she thought I would go off and confront my friend and her grandfather for what they did. I thought the best way to handle it was to play along and let them bury themselves.

We went over to the fire as usual after supper. My friend asked me if we were going for another walk that night. I thanked her for the invitation, but firmly informed her I had other plans. I wish I had a picture of their faces when I announced that I was going to see him again that evening. I thought my friend's eyes would pop; she had them open so wide in surprise. I was glad that I didn't have to say anything more.

I was toying with the idea of waiting to see if he would really come and get me, but game playing time was over. Tonight it would be me, and just me, totally, honestly, from that moment on, no matter what questions he asked. I told everyone I would see them later and started up the road to what I hoped would be a big part of my future.

He was sitting there, by the fire, when I walked up. I couldn't see what he was thinking. He had this far away look in his eyes. I said hello, but hesitated to go any closer until he 'came back' to the park. He sat up and motioned for me to take the seat next to him. It felt so natural to sit there with his arm around me, talking as if we had known each other for years, rather than days. I fit nicely into the curve of his body and his lips were made to move over mine. Or maybe that part was because we practiced so much. I liked everything about this man.

He sat up abruptly, interrupting the conversation we were having, and asked me bluntly how old I was. "I'm a junior in high school," I answered hesitantly.

"That's good. Now, how old are you?"

"Does age really matter?"

"No. How old are you?"

"How old do I look?" I asked. I *really* didn't want to answer that question.

"How old are you?" he asked again, rapidly losing patience.

"I'm sixteen," I answered, bracing myself.

"There, that wasn't so hard, was it?" He settled back into his original position.

There was no explosion. There was no worried look or sudden intake of breath. I didn't know whether to kiss him or smack him and tell him to react rather that sitting there looking at me. I decided a kiss would be better.

"Sweet sixteen and never been kissed," I flirted.

"Well, we'll just have to fix that," he said, and we did.

He pulled back far enough to look at me and asked me a strange question. "Do you want me to stay another night?"

I didn't know what to say. Of course I wanted him to stay another night. I didn't want to have to say goodbye to him, not this early. He just met the real me, 'Well, who's fault is that?' I asked myself. I didn't know how to answer the question and I wanted him to clarify it.

"What do you mean?"

"I only have the campsite until tonight. I could pay for another night and not go home until tomorrow. That means we could spend more time together. But if you'd rather not, I would have to be taking off any minute now."

'Leave any minute?' I thought. I couldn't let go, not yet.

"Will it cost you a lot? Do you have anything to do at home? I don't want you to put off something important." I was grasping at straws and I knew it. I didn't want to come right out and say I wanted him to stay.

"No, I don't have anything more important that this right now," he said, squeezing my hand. "I would just have to call my mother and let her know. She would think I ran off into a ditch if I didn't get home when I usually do."

"Well, let's go make that call!" I was tired of dancing around the subject. I wanted him to stay, and he wanted to stay, was there really anything wrong with coming right out and saying it? I jumped off the bench and grabbed his hand to pull him up as well.

"Wait a minute. I have to lock the truck and get my wallet," he laughed at my anxiousness. Just between you and me, he forgot to luck his truck.

We walked hand in hand up to the telephone. I don't remember what the whole conversation was, but one part I will never forget. He chatted with his mom for a bit; then when his mother apparently asked him why he wasn't coming home, he looked at me and said, "Something just came up," and winked at me. I could imagine what his mother was thinking. If she was at all like mine, she knew exactly what 'something' was.

After he hung up, we walked back to his campsite by the scenic route. We walked down by the river to 'our' spot and all around the park. We talked and talked and laughed and joked. At one point, I was telling a story and, to see his reaction, I was in front of him walking backwards. Story finished, big laugh having been shared, he reached forward and pulled me back to him. At my questioning look, he stated matter-of-factly, "You were entirely too far away."

I steered him around the back of the bathhouse instead of taking the road that lead to my campsite. It's not that I didn't want to rub in the fact that the plan hatched by our neighbors didn't work; I didn't want the hassle of a possible confrontation to ruin a perfectly beautiful evening.

We walked right by his campsite and headed for the beach. By that time of the evening the sun was down and the moon was out. We stood there looking at the stars and the lights of Canada across the waters of the St. Lawrence. I pointed out a few constellations. I don't know if he was impressed by my knowledge, but he seemed interested. He asked what a few stars were, but I sensed he had something else on his mind.

"Is something wrong?" I asked, concerned

"No, nothing wrong, really," he said. "I was just wondering 'Why me'? I mean, of all the guys in this park, why did you have to pick on me?" He stared across the river not looking at me.

"I wasn't picking on you. And I said I was sorry," I said worriedly, wondering to myself if he was changing his mind.

"It's nothing to look so worried about. I'm not changing my mind."

He had read my thoughts. I was getting worried and he was getting philosophical. I felt like a dope.

When I stopped to think about it, I had no answer for his question. I had no idea why I walked up to him that first night and asked him about the jet-ski. I couldn't explain the ease with which we talked to each other. I had no explanation for why his touch burned my skin. I could only sense the cord that was wrapping itself around our hearts. I looked heavenward, praying my thanks.

After watching the stars a few minutes more, we walked back to his campsite one final time, this time with his arm around me, and started a fire. He held me so close. I felt safe and secure. I stopped trying to figure out what he was thinking and purely felt, and enjoyed. Every so often he would squeeze me really tight, to making sure I was really there, not some figment of his imagination, or mine, but a real live person who wanted to be with him.

I thought about how he found out about me, and started to get angry once more. I still didn't know how he was told; I just knew that he was.

"What did my friend's grandfather say to you when he told you about me?" I asked out of the blue.

"He came over and started asking about the jet-ski, then said, 'I hear you have been having lots of company.' I said, 'Yeah, some girl and her foreign exchange student friend.' He said, 'I hate to tell you this, but she's not German. They have been pulling your leg.'"

"'Well,' I thought, 'Let's see just how far she is going to go with this." He turned to me, "That's why I ignored you when you first came over yesterday. I wanted to get rid of you. Then I decided to go along with it and have a laugh behind your back."

"So, you let me make a fool of myself!" I said indignantly.

"Do you want to talk about being made a fool of?" he asked back, mimicking my expression.

"O.K.," I grimaced. I did deserve that. "Why didn't you say anything?"

"I kind of wanted you to tell me. That's why I said you could tell me anything last night. I wanted you to say it." He was looking at me so earnestly; I felt the urge to explain.

"I wanted to tell you. You don't know how much I wanted to tell you. But I thought you would be angry and say you didn't want anything to do with me."

"Angry isn't the word for it. I was down right pissed off! You don't know how close you were to never seeing me again. I was going to pack everything up this morning and leave right after work for home."

"Why didn't you?" I asked, hoping to gain some insight.

"I honestly don't know," he said, shaking his head in disbelief at himself. "I figured I would give you another chance."

"Then I'm glad I wrote the letter." I was really glad I had written that letter!

"I wasn't going to read it," he said, and to my questioning look he answered, "I thought I knew what was in it. But then I decided I better. When I got to the part that you wanted to meet me, I looked at my watch and finished the rest fast. I knew I better get moving if I was going to be on time. I didn't want you to leave before I got there."

"Now aren't you glad you did give me another chance?" I nuzzled a little closer. I thought he would say yes or 'You bet I'm glad' but his answer almost put me into shock.

"I don't know yet. You did cost me another seven bucks. I wonder if you're worth it?"

I felt like getting up and walking away with what little dignity I had left after that humiliating remark, but I settled for smacking him playfully on the arm. Too late I noticed he was joking. If I could have crawled into a hole, I would have.

"Hey!" he said, "I was only kidding." He reached over and rubbed his arm as I apologized over and over.

"It's all right. I deserved that," he said. I felt really bad about what I had done and was still apologizing when he gathered me up in his arms and gave me the most breathtaking kiss I have ever had. I replied in kind and we cuddled together and talked quietly for the rest of the evening. Only one comment stands out in my memory of our various conversations that warm night. He turned to me with great surprise and asked, "Why is it I feel I can tell you anything?"

He walked me home and we had one last sweet kiss. One would have to last us through the long hours of the night before we could see each other again the next morning.

As it was, we were to leave the park the next morning. We packed up the camper and sat around watching the children finish their breakfast before we started the long drive home. I told my aunt about the events of the night before and she looked as if she was remembering the time that led up to she and my uncle falling in love. I asked her if it was all right for me to say goodbye to him and give him my address. She said it was perfectly fine with her, but warned me that 'no matter how perfect last night was, he probably won't write'.

That was an unimaginable thought. I ordered it out of my mind immediately. 'Of course he will write me,' I thought. 'You can't fake what we experienced the last few nights. But writing doesn't amount to a hill of beans if we can't see each other.' I swear, I was shaking when I walked up to him. He gave me the look I will always think of as 'my' look and told me good morning.

"I thought I would come over and say goodbye before you left for home and give you my address and phone number. In case you were bored and wanted to write or call," I said hesitantly.

"I don't have to be bored, do I?" he asked, always the kidder.

'No, but I must warn you, my letters just ramble on at times," I said, hoping he wanted me to write him, too. 'What are you thinking?' I scolded myself. 'If he is going to write you, he would be expecting a letter back.' I called myself a few choice words, that I would rather not repeat, and concentrated on what he was saying.

We chatted lightly while exchanging addresses and numbers, then the time came to go. I saw my uncle pulling his truck up in front of the camper in preparation to hook it on and knew it must be time to go. I helped him put his folded tent in the back of his truck, after he kiddingly told me to stop watching him and give him a hand, and we kissed. I don't know what he was thinking; but I didn't want to let go, and told him so.

"Well, you are going to have to, I have to get moving. It's one long drive and I have had a few late nights lately," he smiled light-heartedly.

I honestly thought I would start crying. I know he thought the same thing because he hastened to add, "This isn't the last time you'll see me. You live by a lake, don't you? Maybe I'll bring the jet-ski up and show you how to ride it next weekend. How's that sound?"

It sounded wonderful. I thought I would have to wait weeks until I saw him again, and he was already making plans for the next weekend. I swore to myself that, even if this was just another summer romance, I wasn't going to over-analyze or read too much into the situation. I was going to enjoy every second of how much, or how little, we had. I kept my promise faithfully—until he moved to get into his truck. We both waved as he drove away.

Chapter Four

The ride home was just as uneventful as the ride up was: more potty stops and more snack breaks. I mainly stared out the window and dreamed, or rather, remembered. I tried to think of something interesting to write to him about. I could tell him the whole saga of the ride home. 'What are you thinking?' I chided myself. 'Let him write first, then all you have to do is answer.' That was a brilliant idea, until the camper was unloaded and the children were napping. I was so bored; I actually dusted picture frames to keep busy. I decided I would talk to him in my letter as if he was right here with me, that way, maybe, I wouldn't miss him so much. 'These next two weeks are going to crawl by,' I thought.

By the following Sunday night, I couldn't take it anymore. I had written him fifteen drafts of the same letter, mailed one, and then copied it over and over to have something to do. I dug into my purse and found his telephone number. I just looked at it for the longest time. Then, I dialed. 'My mother would skin me alive if she knew I was doing the calling,' I laughed to myself. My mother was very old fashioned in her thinking. I knew there was no sense in bringing anyone home to meet her if she was going to throw him out anyways. It made me more selective with my escorts.

The phone rang three times before someone answered. I asked if he was there. They said, "Just a second," and hollered his name. I could hear voices in the background, but couldn't make out any words. Then, I heard his voice on the line. "Hello."

"Hi! How have you been?" I asked nervously, hoping he would recognize my voice. My hopes came true and my heart soared as he started talking like a week hadn't gone by since we saw each other.

"I have been fine, been doing a lot of work."

"Nothing too strenuous, I hope. You know how old bones can be," I kidded him. He was only eight years older than I was, but he was always calling himself an old man.

"Ha, ha," he said, "What have you been up to?"

"Nothing really. Here's a funny story for you. I was trying to bake brownies, but something happened to one of the children and, as I was kissing a boo-boo, they burned. I felt so bad. I don't think anyone is going to eat them." I finished the last quickly. I didn't know what else to say and I knew I was rambling. I couldn't seem to stop myself.

"I don't blame them if they didn't," he laughed.

"Well, I'll just tell them they are German style," I laughed, so glad he hadn't taken my rambling seriously.

"That's cute, I've got to remember that." He sounded strained, like someone was right there listening.

"You can't really talk, can you?" I asked bluntly.

"No, not really, but I sure am going to give it a try," he laughed. Yep, there was someone listening, but it wasn't going to stop him. I liked that. He wasn't afraid of 'us' and wanted to keep us out in the open. After being a 'hidden' girlfriend, that simple act meant the world to me. I was relieved he didn't want to hang up, not yet.

"I got your letter," he said during a lull in the conversation.

"You did? When? Could you read my writing?" I was so excited that he had actually read it. I couldn't stop my excitement from bubbling over.

"It was here when I got here, and I could read it fine," he laughed, my enthusiasm infecting him also. "The way you wrote it, it was almost like I could hear your voice. I must be crazy." I could picture him shaking his head at his last statement.

"You're not crazy. I wrote it that way on purpose. I write all my letters that way, it makes me feel closer just to think I'm talking to you." I paused for a minute, then cautiously asked if he had written me yet.

"Yes, I did. It should get there tomorrow or the next day. I mailed it Thursday. Listen, in your letter you said something about wanting to go see a concert at the state fair. I'd like to take you, if you still want to go," his voice sounded shaky. He was actually nervous that I might say that I didn't want to go with him. The realization astonished me. I had only mentioned the concert in passing in my letter, but he had picked up on it. I was still basking in the moment of being foremost in his thoughts when I realized he still was waiting for my answer. Too shocked to say anything else, I vaguely said I was still planning to go, then changed the subject.

We talked for a few minutes more, about the next weekend and what we were going to do. I told him I would send him directions, and he said he would call before he left to let me know around what time he would get to my house. We reluctantly said goodbye and hung up.

It was only a telephone call, but he was right next to me again. I had called him so I wouldn't miss him so much and only succeeded in missing him more. I took out my notebook and wrote him a three page letter, including very explicit directions to my house. I did not want him to get lost!

I went to bed that night with what I can only describe as a warm feeling in my heart. It was only five days until I saw him again.

The next morning I was glued to the window through which you could see the mailbox. I had put my letter in it to go out to him, and was hoping I would find one from him in its place. The mailman drove up, stopped, then drove away. When he was safely out of sight, I dashed out of the house and fairly knocked the mailbox over trying to get inside it. It was there. I hadn't realized I was holding my breath until I let it out in a big sigh.

I took the letter into the house and sat there for a minute looking at his handwriting. I turned it over and opened it. Inside had to be one of the most ridiculous letters I have ever read; but it was from him, to me. It mostly talked about what he did during the week. He dated each entry like a diary and he wrote a little every day. I couldn't believe how much we had in common even in our letter writing style. For instance, in my letter I apologized for the mess, and in his he said, 'I'm just now looking back over what I've been writing for the last few days and would like to wish you luck in reading it'. Later, he threatens to fire his pencil for bad penmanship.

I could tell by the way he was writing how he felt at the time of day it was. He was really happy at the beginning of the week; but near the end he got a little depressed. What caught my heart was

a little note he slipped in on a scrap of paper. 'Hint #1 Being an average American male, I sometimes have a hard time expressing myself and my feelings. The songs mentioned happen to be saying the thing I think I'd like to say.'
I read back over the letter, this time noting the songs and where they were put.

Among the many things we had in common, the most ironic was his little sister's name was the same as mine. He and she were very close. He told me in his letter that he had told her about me, but not his mother. I thought that was great! I have older brothers and I wished they would confide in me. Just by the way he talked; I could tell their family had a special relationship.

I read and reread his letter before I sat down to write him another one. 'I sure hope he wasn't going to be shy about getting mail,' I thought. I looked at the clock and suddenly realized that I would see him in four days. It didn't seem so long, now that I had something from him to hold on to. I only wanted to keep busy and not waste time missing him when I couldn't make time move any faster.

Saturday morning dawned bright and beautiful. My excitement and nervousness kept me up most of the night and didn't get a very restful sleep when I did manage to doze off. I got up and took my time in the shower. I wanted everything to be perfect.

I started packing for the beach, towels and such, when I noticed my bikini on my dresser. I bought it in the spring as a gag to show my mother, just to see her face, and had packed it to move to my aunt's for the summer. I debated for a minute. 'What type of signal would that suit give?' I jokingly asked myself. I grabbed it and threw it into my beach bag. If he wanted to see me, I would sure give him an eyeful in that suit. I didn't think I would have the courage to wear it, but I wanted to be prepared.

The phone rang exactly when he had said it would, like he was waiting on his end of the line for the right second to call. It's comical, but I don't remember much about the call. The only thing I do recall with perfect clarity is the way his voice sounded when we were hanging up. He sounded sad and hopeful, both at the same time.

"I'll see you in two hours," he said. He sounded, well, nervous.

'Why would he be nervous? He had nothing to be nervous about, right? I should be shaking like a leaf. I'm the one thinking of wearing that bikini in public,' I puzzled. I could not make my mind wrap around the thought that he was scared of anything, much less seeing me. I shrugged the feeling off and pondered what I would do for the next two hours.

As it turned out, I didn't have to decide. My aunt and uncle wanted to do some shopping and other running around before I left. The two hours passed quickly enough, although I managed to look at the clock every two minutes while playing with the children. Now, as I look back on that day, I don't think my aunt had any shopping to do. It's hard to go shopping and not have any bags when you return. I think she wanted to give us a couple of minutes to ourselves, properly chaperoned by the kids, before he had to meet my uncle. All men are nervous, if not down-right scared, to meet the dominant male figure in their girlfriend's life. Usually a father would do, but in this specific case, my uncle could accomplish the intimidation nicely. Did I say girlfriend?

He pulled in the driveway a few minutes after the prospective two hours and beeped. I couldn't run out and hop in the truck and take off. I motioned for him to come in. He waved back and started for the house. Later, I was to learn the beep was accidental.

I had always thought the door to the house was plenty big enough for anything, until I saw him framed in the doorway. Everything seemed dwarfed by his size. I still couldn't get over the ease with which he moved for a man that tall.

I wanted to hold him, and have him hold me. The only problem was I didn't know how to make that happen. A friend of my brother's was always saying, 'Ask and ye shall receive.'

"Can I have a hug?" I asked, hoping I wouldn't seem desperate.

He said something to the effect of "Sure," and enfolded me in a big bear hug. When I felt his arms relax, I looked up and saw he had his eyes closed and was leaning forward. I stood up on my toes and gave him a long awaited kiss.

I remembered my manners and offered him a seat. We looked at my tapes and he kidded me about my taste in music. My older cousin was a real rough-houser and jumped all over him. I don't think he minded because he gave as good as he got. I like watching them play around, but I thought I saw an uneasy note in his eyes. 'He can't still be nervous,' I thought. 'He's here at least, and I intend to make this a day to remember!'

My aunt and uncle returned a few minutes later. They chatted with him, asked the usual questions. He passed their 'test'. I was caught off guard when they asked where we were going. I still didn't know where we were going myself. I asked him what he needed to put the jet-ski in the water hoping that would give me some clue. All he needed was a beach, he said, Where was a good place?

I decided we should probably go to a beach I knew near a campground right on the edge of the lake. It was in the middle of a deep spot in the lake; close enough to the road that we could see the truck;

and it didn't have five miles of hot sand to walk over to get to the water. He was saying goodbye to my aunt and uncle when I snapped out of my thoughts. I grabbed my beach bag and followed him out of the house. My aunt said something about, if we missed curfew, they would come looking for us with one of my uncle's guns. He laughed when he heard that.

He opened my door for me, then got into the truck himself. 'They're going to get along,' I thought, silently saying a prayer of thanks. As he backed out of the driveway, I happened to look back at the house windows and noticed my aunt had seen him open my door. I noticed the 'thumbs-up' sign she gave me too.

We drove down to the beach by the scenic route. The day was gorgeous. The sun couldn't have shown any brighter or any warmer if I had special ordered it from God himself.

For conversation's sake, I complimented him on his truck. It was really nice inside and had a great stereo system. He blasted the tunes and we laughed as the old couple on the corner gave us an annoyed look.

The beach wasn't crowded, so he pulled the truck over on the side of the road and parked right next to the beach. I excused myself to go change, but before I did, I offered to help him with the jet-ski.

"I can handle it all right. I'm used to throwing this thing around," he joked.

I crossed the road to the bath house, and inside began my dilemma. I pulled out the one-piece bathing suit I brought and looked at it with disdain. It was a very simple suit. It had rainbow colors and the straps ran up my shoulders and crossed in the back. I couldn't see me making a big entrance in that suit. It looked like a suit a twelve-year-old would wear! I did not want to remind him of my age any more than necessary. I dug around in my bag and found the bikini. It wasn't especially revealing. I had been choosey when buying it. I must have tried on fifty suits in the store to find the right one. It couldn't be too tight or loose; I didn't want body parts falling out. But I also wanted a suit that would flatter my shape. I finally settled on a white suit with pink stripes that tied behind my neck and back. The bottom wasn't cut very high, just enough to give my legs the look they were longer and slimmer than they already were.

I took my time putting it on, making sure all the strings were tied tightly. The suit falling off wasn't the only problem. The genuine problem came when I started to walk out of the bathroom. I didn't know how to make the walk across the road. I wanted to get, and keep, his attention; not everyone's on the beach. I pulled my beach towel out of my bag and slung it over my shoulder. I held my beach bag in the other hand, gritted my teeth, then walked bravely over to where he had taken the jet-ski off the truck.

He was bending down untying something and looked up when he heard me walking toward him. He had a look on his face of shock and delight. I had the effect I desired, now to move in for the kill. I tossed my bag into the passenger side of the truck, took my towel off my shoulder, and dragged it behind me as I walked back over to him.

I nonchalantly said something about wondering if the water was cold and he looked up at me again. This time, his eyes followed over the length of me from my bare feet to the smile on my face. I couldn't see his eyes because he quickly looked back down to finish untying his sneakers, but I could read his body language. His whole body suddenly went tense and I knew my plan worked. I'm no moron about how the male ego works, and I wasn't then.

I didn't want to give him a complex or anything, so I put my towel back over my shoulder and walked around on the sand while he finished putting the jet-ski into the water.

I followed him out into the water a short way and listened to him as he explained how it worked and balance on it. He put his life jacket on and took off riding around. He splashed some people who had swum out to the sandbar and were messing around. I swam around a little, but mostly I just stood there, watching him fall off and get back on, shivering. I didn't know it until later, but he was just showing off, again.

I started to get worried that he would take off and leave me there alone. He didn't know the area that well from the water and he would probably end up on the other side of the lake out of gas or something. All my worries were for nothing because, a few minutes later, he came back and splashed me as he went by. I tried to duck under water, but not in time. Most of the water hit me right in the face.

I came back to the surface to find him laughing. I splashed him back and soon we were in the midst of a water fight. He swam underwater to where I was, surfaced just in front of me, grabbed a quick kiss, then back under water to swim away. I finally caught up to him and dunked him under before he saw me coming.

"That was for getting me with the jet-ski!" I laughed as he sputtered, trying to get the water out of his eyes.

We played around, hanging onto the jet-ski to keep afloat and chatting. He told me a joke about a halibut and another about a pig. They weren't funny; but I was so happy, I laughed anyway. He tried to teach me how to ride the jet-ski, the key word there being tried, before he took off one more time. I walked back to the beach to dry off. I was sitting on a towel when he came back to the beach.

He asked me if I wanted to go; but I assured him he could keep riding as long as he wanted to, I was just cold. He pulled the jet-ski out of the water and loaded it onto the truck. I started walking over to the bathhouse to change when he told me to wait and show him the way. Inside, I took off my bikini, thanked it, wrapped it in the towel, then shoved it in my beach bag. He was waiting for me when I came out. He offered me his hand and we walked together back to the truck. He opened the door for me, ever the gentleman, then stole a kiss before I could get in. He drove off to find a good restaurant for lunch.

We decided to go to an Italian place on the main street of the town. It was a pleasant enough lunch. I was uneasy about eating pizza in front of him. If I may interject one word of advice: do not have pizza for dinner on the first date.

After leaving a tip for the waitress, he said he wanted to look around town. It was a beach town and it was packed with shops and an amusement park. We walked back to the truck and made sure the jet-ski was all right, then strolled around. We wandered into a couple shops and he looked at t-shirts. I followed him, watching him, learning about him. We sometimes held hands, and sometimes not. I sensed he knew that all he would have to do was turn around, and there I would be.

I knew the town better than he did so I suggested that we get the truck and park it by the amusement park so we wouldn't have to walk the entire way back across town when we left.

At the amusement park, he was hilarious. My sides hurt from laughing so much. He would stop at every game to check out the prizes and tell me what the 'catch' was. He found fault with every ride; this went too fast, this went too slow. If he was looking to me for ideas or hints of something I wanted to do, I'm afraid he was lost. I was doing what I wanted, looking at him looking at me. I could have been in heaven and never noticed the change.

We walked out to the beach and started out to the pier when he noticed a boat going by and stopped to watch it. It was an effortless thing, but standing there, with his arm around me, made me feel like a queen. It is difficult to describe the way my heart swelled to accommodate all the feelings I had for this man. I wouldn't call it love… Yes, I would. But I couldn't call it that…yet. I wanted to try to hold onto my resolution not to over analyze our relationship and just enjoy how much, or how little, we had.

We wandered over to the edge of the beach where the rocks were and watched the sun set. It was the perfect ending to the perfect day. It was so beautiful. We just sat there. We didn't talk or even look at each other for the longest time. When his fingers started drawing little circles on my shoulder, I turned to him and met his lips in a kiss. We sat there kissing as people walked by and the sun finished setting.

We walked to his truck and talked even more. I look back on that day and it seems all we did was talk, and kiss. He explained to me that he didn't mean to beep when he pulled into the driveway. He was still shaking from the drive up and hit the horn by mistake as he turned the wheel. I couldn't leave a comment like that alone.

"Why were you shaking?" I asked innocently. "Was the traffic that bad on the drive up? Or was a big, strong guy like you nervous about seeing li'l ol' me?"

He looked at me, shaking his head, "Whew,

yeah, I was nervous," he admitted.

He was so adorable and uncomfortable. I had the answer I was looking for, so I decided to let him off the hook.

"As nervous as I was in that bikini?" I giggled as I asked. "You should have seen the look on your face when I walked up to you. Did I surprise you?"

"Surprised isn't the word for it," he looked out the window as he continued. "I mean, a day at the beach, I knew I'd see you in a swim suit. Then you come walking out in that!"

He turned to me with a look so cryptic, I was immediately fearful. I needed clarification for a comment like that. "And? What did you think? How'd I look?" I asked, holding my breath. I wanted him to be honest, always, but a bad review would have devastated me.

"You looked great!" was his response. He looked me over from head to toe, remembering the sight, then turned back out the window, rubbing his forehead and smiling.

"Really?" I didn't mean to ask that out loud, but I was so relieved I couldn't stop myself.

He looked back at me and took my face in his hands. "You're beautiful and you know it," he admitted. His eyes told me everything I had wanted to know. I smiled a little smile watching the emotions play across his face. Seeing this, his eyes scanned over my face and back to my lips.

"Hm-mm," he sighed, as if the last grip he had on his emotions was gone and he was asking himself, 'Yup, I'm wrapped around her finger. Now what?' A slow, emotional kiss was what he came up with.

We watched the boat traffic along the canal and I told him about my family, which could get confusing. We talked about the courses I was planning to take in the fall and plans for the future. I was already taking college classes and would be set up nicely to get my degree from my favorite college, financial aid and all. He loved to chide me about my foreign language studies.

"Geesh, you're a brain! What do you find so interesting about me?" he asked suddenly.

I wasn't sure how to answer that question. I could have given him a funny answer to lighten the mood, but by the look in his eyes I knew he needed something to calm his insecurities.

"I don't really know." I started out loud, but in my mind I was making a list: the way you look at me; the way you make me feel; the electric shock whenever you're near me; everything we have in common; the fact that I can be absolutely perfectly naturally myself with you. "There is just something about you. Maybe it's your eyes. Even if you don't say a word, I know what you're thinking."

"Oh really? What am I thinking now?" he asked jokingly.

I leaned forward and gave him a quick kiss.

"Close," he said with his eyes still closed, "very close."

I leaned forward again and kissed him with all the passion he had awakened in me. I couldn't believe the flood of emotions that ran through me as our lips moved together. I surrendered to each and every one. I leaned back just far enough to see his eyes.

"Close," he began again, but was cut off when I pushed him back against the door of the truck. We both looked at each other and burst out laughing. Every time one would look at the other, we start laughing all over again. We must have laughed for a full five minutes before we managed to calm down.

By then the dusk of the evening had turned into the dark of night. However, parked under a street light like we were, it was not the mood he was looking for. He started the engine of the truck and drove around looking for make-out spots. He laughed when he told me he used to drive around on weekends and shine his lights on the couples who were necking at those spots in his home town. Because, he said, he didn't date much, which I thought was a ludicrous, and didn't have anything else to do. We drove around in back of the school and were going to park when he noticed a car pulling in behind us.

"I hope it's not a cop," I prayed out loud.

"It is," he said, putting the truck in reverse. He was going to back up when the cop started getting out of his car. The cop walked over and talked to him for a minute. From my side of the truck I couldn't hear what was being said. After a second, he started laughing and the cop got back in his car and drove away.

"What did he say?" I asked.

"Not much," he said, paying attention to driving out of the parking lot. "He just said that I didn't look like the type to vandalize the school." He laughed again and said, "If he only knew."

After that close call, we drove out into the country for a few miles and he pulled over to the side of the road.

"It's not exactly secluded, but it's out of the way," he said, taking the truck out of gear and parking. His hands absolutely fascinated me. They were so large and strong they could easily toss around the firewood at the campground, yet touch me so gently I had no will of my own. They were always warm and when he put them on my shoulders to pull me towards him I was obliged to comply. I realized I would go wherever those hands would take me. 'Where you lead, I will follow,' I promised him in my thoughts. I loved him. At that minute, I knew I had fallen in love with the man of my dreams. Whether I couldn't, wouldn't, or shouldn't say it out loud, I knew it. That realization was as remarkable as it was frightening.

We drove back down to the beach to

check out the night-life there. As usual, my impulsiveness took over and I thanked him for not trying anything more than kissing. He looked at me with 'my' look and asked why.

Things were getting too serious and I needed to make a joke quick to make amends for my outlandish comment. "Don't you think it would have been a little cramped in here?" I joked, waving a hand around the truck.

He laughed, but suddenly got quiet. "I could tell you something that would explain why I didn't try anything, but I don't know if I should," he said after a minute of silence.

I thought I would lighten the mood, but now it was more serious that it was before. "You told me I could tell you anything and you would understand. Why don't you try it yourself? I will understand."

"I didn't try anything because I've never had sex before. I probably wouldn't know how to try anything."

I had no idea what to expect, but I sure wasn't expecting that confession. That changed everything. It put our relationship into perspective.

I mean, most relationships followed a certain pattern. You meet, you like each other, you date and usually sleep together shortly thereafter. I have to admit, I was relieved. Now I wouldn't have to worry about what to do or say if that awkward situation ever came up. I wanted an 'adult' relationship with him, but I didn't want to jump into bed with the man to prove it.

"It's nothing to be ashamed or embarrassed about. I think that's a noble quality." I was trying to assure him that I did understand like he asked, but only succeeded in putting my foot in my mouth...again.

"I'm not embarrassed or ashamed, I just don't go around advertising it! And I wasn't trying to be noble, I just always thought there were more important things in a relationship than that and never pushed the issue." He said it so firmly that I was scared to say another word. I knew I had to say something, but I had to choose my words carefully. He was embarrassed and looking for a way out of this conversation. I decided to say the two words he had wanted to hear in the first place.

"I understand." There. Simply put, direct,

and to the point.

"O.k.," he said as we pulled into my driveway. He turned off the truck and quickly looked at me. "I'm sorry; but I didn't intend to tell you that and I guess I just over-reacted. Why do I feel like I can tell you anything?"

I looked at him like he was the silliest man on the face of the earth. "I know. I should have just said, 'I understand' in the first place and left it at that."

"Can you forgive me?" we both asked each other at the same time, then burst out laughing. It was such a silly thing; we couldn't help laughing.

I invited him in for a bit because I saw my uncle looking out the kitchen window. Inside, he swore he was just checking to see who had pulled in the driveway and not checking to see what we were up to. This made us all laugh and changed the mood to a more relaxed atmosphere. They asked us the usual questions: where did we go and what did we do? We visited until he noticed the time and said good-bye to them. I walked him out to his truck, not wanting to miss a single second of time together. I was just going to say a quick goodbye when he pulled me into his arms and gently kissed me. He worriedly and hopefully asked me about the fair and concert. I told him one of my best friends was having a birthday the night before. Why didn't he meet me there? I could stay at her house, and he in a motel like he did when he worked out of town anyways, then we could leave the next morning and spend the whole day together.

"That way it would save you some travel time," I finished.

"Sounds O.K. to me," he sighed a big sigh of relief. "You'll have to send me directions, though. You know my memory; I'll forget it by the time I get to the end of the road." He was always joking about his memory, or rather his lack of one.

"As long as you don't forget me, it's all right," I chanced a small declaration.

"I could never forget you that easy," he laughed.

"And are you planning to?" I asked, when he stopped laughing. After he shook his head, I continued confidently, "That's good, because now that you got me, you're going to have one hell of a time getting rid of me."

"Is that so?" he asked, raising an eyebrow. "Are you that possessive?"

"Yes, I'm very possessive. I'm not possessive the way I get things, but I'm very possessive the way I keep things. Well, you know what I mean, I hope?" I finished, realizing I was rambling.

"Yes, I think I do." He nodded and tightened his arms around me. "Well, it is a long drive home and I should be getting going."

I didn't want the night to end but he was right. It was a long drive back to his house, and he had a long day of jet-skiing planned for the next day with his jet-ski club.

We kissed again and again, both knowing it would have to last until the next weekend. He got into his truck and drove away. I walked into the dark house and felt my way to my bedroom, put my nightgown on and tried to get some sleep, all the while reliving the whole day in my mind.

Chapter Five

I had a lot to think about the following week. Not simply to occupy my thoughts, but to work out as well. I was sure we had a 'real' relationship, but how much and of what kind? I knew sex wouldn't be an issue, and I was glad of that. There was so much going on in my heart that was one less thing to worry about. It brought what we had to a different level. It made the feelings somehow more true and sincere knowing they weren't guided by mere physical attraction. The attraction was there, don't get me wrong. I wasn't dismissing that aspect, just putting it off.

I got another letter from him during the week that laid my fears to rest. He did the cutest thing at the beginning and end of every letter. He would write 'This is letter A', or whatever letter we were up to, 'The first letter of our alphabet'. Then he would write 'Look for letter B coming to a PO box near you soon' at the end of every letter. I don't think that would be so important coming from any other person. Other than that, he just asked for directions. He had no way of knowing I had sent them to him the day after the beach. I would read and reread his letters over and over when I would miss him, which was almost every hour.

What's more, I had to think about what category of future we would have together. He was eight years older than me and had done or experienced numerous things I was still dreaming about. He had gone to college, had a good job with a firm background, and had responsibilities. He had a truck payment, gas, taxes and bosses to worry about.

It was easy to say that our age difference didn't matter in the privacy of his truck or tucked away in a secluded part of a beach. But what would happen when we brought our feelings out into practical, everyday situations?

I knew my friends would accept him. I had already written to my closest friends and told them about it. The response totally floored me. They all thought I was taking a *huge* chance, but told be to 'go for it' and chase happiness.

My biggest fear was his friends and family. They had grown up with him and knew him much better. They could probably take one look at me and tell me the future of this impossible relationship. This is precisely what happens with any family. I knew I would have to keep a cool head when I met them, but to be myself and let them get to know the girl he felt close enough with to confide the utmost personal secrets.

We all, each of us, deny that anyone else's opinion matters but our own. It is much nicer when the closest people to you approve of and accept the person you are in love with. He and I were no different. We both needed to have the support and respect of our families.

I was scared. Plain and simple terrified to make a bad impression on his family. I had heard him talk about them, knew they were all close, knew his views on family and friends. I knew that I would most likely meet a few members of his family at the fair. He had written to me in his second letter that his mother and younger sister had plans to attend the same concert we were going to. An introduction was inevitable.

My aunt and uncle dropped me off at my friend's house, which by the way, was directly the other end of my hometown where I lived with my mother. I ran into the house, eager to catch up on all the gossip I missed so far over the summer, and hugged my friend. Her boyfriend was there playing cards with her parents. I looked at the scene and prayed that when my boyfriend met my parents they would get along like this. I knew I would see him in a couple hours and there was no sense torturing myself.

We were hanging out talking when he drove up. My friend's mother noticed a truck pulling up and asked if anyone knew who this was. I jumped up and ran out to meet him. He was walking towards the house and when he saw me, a big smile of relief spread across his face. I thought it was relief that he had found the right house, but his eyes said once again he was nervous about seeing me.

We hugged and managed to catch a quick kiss before my friend, who had followed me out of the house, raced up behind us and demanded an introduction. He laughed at her enthusiasm and shook his head at me. We walked back into the house and, after introductions all around, sat down to decided what to do that night. Incidentally, this is the first time I introduced him as my boyfriend. My friend decided she wanted to go bowling. I learned a lot that evening, and I'm not talking about him teaching me how to keep score.

After we left the bowling alley, we didn't head right back to my friend's house. We picked up our concert tickets and I showed him where I lived. He said something about definitely having to remember that house. I laughed as we drove by. There was something so exhilarating about just sitting by his side. We were holding hands, but not touching other than that. It was enough for me to notice how tense he was.

We eventually met the others back at my friend's house, but he seemed reluctant to go in. I stayed outside and asked him if anything was wrong.

"Not wrong, really. I just have a few insecurities that are very powerful now. I'm not sure what to do about them." He was noticeably trembling and I had no idea how to handle him. I knew after the evening we had just spent together that he wasn't thinking of telling me he didn't want to see me anymore, but I knew it was something on that level of seriousness.

"I wrote you a letter explaining it all, but

now I don't know if I should give it to you," he said. I reached up and gave him a kiss. I felt his arms encircle me and he held my close for just an instant before a car drove by. We were standing in my friend's front yard, after all. It was so easy to forget about everything else when we were holding each other.

I took a step back and looked up at him with my eyes totally unmasked, hoping he would read the love in them and said, "Remember? Anything in the world and I will understand." I said it very quietly and deliberately, making sure he heard every word.

"O.k.," he said and took my hand to lead me to the truck. Inside, he reached above the visor and took down some folded papers. "Here goes nothing," he said as he handed me the papers.

I unfolded them, then reluctantly looked down to read them. Reluctantly because I was more concerned with reading his eyes than what was written on the papers. I was getting conflicting signals and decided I better read the letter. It would shed some light on the subject.

I couldn't believe my eyes. I was reading

exactly what I had been thinking the past week. 'What's going on? Work's out and boredom is setting in. It's not that I don't have anything to do (ie. Jet-ski, dinner, report to write, etc.) it's that I have no one to do them with. I guess my state of mind is about twenty-five percent boredom and seventy-five percent depression. I need something, I'd rather not say what, because you can't or shouldn't give it yet. My dreams and hopes seem to be a lot like yours. I don't want to say good-bye to you and I need to know how you feel (the truth, no holding back, all out, seriously, in all confidence, straight off the cuff).

Near the end of the letter he goes on: 'To summarize—I don't want to end this relationship, contrary to popular demand. What I want is to know what and how much relationship there is. Help me, please!!'

I folded the letter and looked up at him slowly. I didn't know what to say. I didn't want to say good-bye, either, but just saying it like that wouldn't set aside his fears and insecurities, would it? I must have sat there and thought for what must have felt like an eternity for him because he turned away from me and grabbed the steering wheel with both hands. It looked like he would tear it from the dashboard in his frustration if I didn't say something soon.

"I don't want to say goodbye, either. Right now, I don't *ever* want to say goodbye." There, I said it. I could only hope it worked.

"I knew I shouldn't have given you that damn letter," he began, before he realized what I had said. In the time it takes a heart to beat, what I had said sunk in and he wrapped me up in those arms.

"Aren't you glad you did?" I tried to ask. He was holding me so close that it was very difficult to breathe much less talk. I decided the time for talk was over and I hugged him back.

"Yes," he said when he finally let me go. "I am glad. I didn't know what to expect, but I'm glad to hear you feel the same way that I do. I wasn't so sure there for a while." He looked so relieved sitting there, happily smiling.

"You never have to be unsure again. I know what you mean when you said our dreams seem to be a lot alike. It's eerie sometimes when you think about all the things we have in common." He nodded, eagerly agreeing with me as I went on. "But could you do yourself and me a big favor? Don't over-analyze the situation. My father gave me that advice a long time ago, and it really works. There is no quicker way to ruin a relationship that reading too much into it by over-analyzing it. Just enjoy it!" There, I had said it, passed on my paternal wisdom and hoped he would take it.

"O.K.," he said, waiting impatiently for me to finish. I hadn't realized how fast I was rambling on until I stopped and was out of breath. He was looking at me with a silly look on his face and I knew he wasn't taking me seriously. He looked ready to burst out laughing and I realized I had just made a big fool out of myself. I couldn't face him. I turned away and commented how nice the night was.

"Yes, it is a nice night. I hope tomorrow will be as nice a day as today was."

Why were we sitting there talking about the weather when we had just had a breakthrough in our relationship? 'What the hell happened?' I asked myself. I thought I might cry if he didn't say something soon. We just found out each other's feelings, and we were sitting there like two strangers discussing the weather.

Maybe he wasn't as secure as I was with our feelings and was uncomfortable with them hanging in the air like that. What was I talking about? I wasn't secure with them either and felt uncomfortable. This was a learning experience for both of us.

He touched my shoulder and I almost jumped out the door I was leaning against. I hadn't looked at him since I turned away. I could feel the heat where he had touched slowly burn its way up my neck, turning my head as if I had no will of my own. My eyes were drawn to his and I saw there a look of guilt. 'What was he guilty of?' I asked myself. Could he be having second thoughts already? I wasn't more than fifteen minutes ago he said he didn't want to say goodbye.

"Oh, come on, you look like you're going to cry," he said and brushed the back of his hand across my cheek. "I didn't mean to be so insensitive. I didn't know you were being serious. I was just waiting for you to stop talking so I could kiss you. I didn't want you to get mad at me. It's very good advice and thank your father for giving it to you. Just don't cry!"

Now he was the one talking fast. He sounded so desperate to make up for something he didn't really do. I was the one who misunderstood, and here he was begging me not to burst into tears. He had pulled me to him as he said the last and was running his hand down my hair in a vain attempt to soothe me. I couldn't help myself, but I started laughing.

"Now what?" he asked, sounding very confused and a little annoyed.

"We make one hell of a couple," I managed between giggles. Now I really had him confused. He just sat there looking at me like I had suddenly sprung antlers out of my head.

"I'm not mad at you or anything. When you didn't say anything when I finished, I realized I was rambling and felt really embarrassed. I turned away because you had this look of disbelief on your face and I thought I had made a fool out of myself. I wasn't upset with anybody but myself." I was surprised I could get out that much and laugh hysterically at the same time. I think he was too, because he looked heavenward as if asking for strength.

"And what was this about waiting for me to stop talking before you could kiss me? Since when do you have to wait for anything to kiss me? If you want to, just—" I never got to finish my sentence. He leaned forward and kissed me so fast I never saw it coming.

"You talk too much," he said in between kisses. If it was up to me, we would have kissed all night. Besides, we were getting good at it.

"Just one more thing," he said.

'Uh, oh. Now what?' it was my turn to ask myself.

"But first, I need some air. Look what you did. You're fogging up my windows," he kidded as he opened the door. He held out his hand to help me and I scooted across the seat to get out his door.

"Are you ready?" he asked. After I nodded, he continued. "Did you understand what I meant about wanting something you can't or shouldn't give yet?"

"I was kind of confused, but I figured it

must be one of two things. One could be sex—"

"I thought I told you that wasn't an issue!" he interrupted.

"—or," I continued, "it could mean my feelings for you. Are you afraid I don't mean them?" How could he have thought I didn't mean them?

"I'm not scared that you mean them. I'm glad you mean them. And a little relieved. But you're only sixteen! That's too young to be tied down to one guy. Hell, I'm twenty-four and I think I'm too young to be tied down."

"Is that what you think? That you're tied down?" I asked incredulously. I could not believe what I was hearing.

"Not tied down, exactly, but you know what I mean." He was struggling for the right words to communicate clearly.

It finally hit me like a ton of bricks. 'Tied down' wasn't the phrase in his statement that was key, it was the 'only sixteen' part.

"Is that what is bothering you? If my age matters that much to you, why don't we just call the whole thing off!" I was so frustrated I remember shouting at him. I was doomed. No matter which way I turned. Either my age mattered and nothing I ever said to him would be taken seriously, because obviously sixteen-year-olds were too immature to know what they wanted out of life or whom to share it with or make any life changing decisions, which is what he was asking me to do. Or it didn't matter, and he was still asking me to make a life changing decision that he was going to argue with anyway. I turned around to leave him there and go back into the house.

I didn't even get two steps when he grabbed my arm and turned me back to him. He was holding both of my arms and had that fierce look on his face that I hadn't seen since the night in the state park when he said I could tell him anything.

"It's not your age. I don't care how old you are!" He was fighting to find the right words again. "It's just that, I *know* what I'm doing. I'm sure! Are you?" he prayed. "I just want you to be sure."

After everything we had said throughout the evening, he wouldn't be totally confident unless I said the exact words.

"Yes, I'm sure," I said. I didn't have to say

anything else. I never had the chance, even if I wanted to. After he heard my breathless reply, he pulled me into his arms in a bone crushing hug. I didn't mind, though. I still couldn't believe what had just happened. It was continually incomprehensible how, in all the world, we were standing in each other's arms. There is no place I would rather have been.

The next morning I woke up not having slept at all. I was still in a daze from the last night's events and couldn't wait to start the day. My friend, her brother, and I drew straws to see who would get the shower first. I'm glad I won, because, not five minutes after I finished drying my hair, he drove up to the house.

I met him outside for a quick kiss before being engulfed in the activity of the house. He told me he wanted to change the plans we had made the night before. He wanted to go back to his house so he could drop off the jet-ski, which was still on the back of his truck, and we could go to mass there, then fair and concert. It sounded great to me so I went back into the house, grabbed my suitcase, told my friend about the change of plans, and made

arrangements to meet them all later at the fair. I
gave him directions out of town towards the
highway and we were off.

The ride down to his house was more than
two hours. We talked about everything, as usual,
but I was so nervous about meeting his family that
the closer we got to his house, the more I shook. He
smiled when he noticed this and told me not to
worry, the only family there would probably be his
parents and younger sister. 'Great,' I thought, 'the
three people I am most unprepared for, I am to meet
today.' I looked down at what I was wearing and
almost begged him to pull over so I could change.
What I was wearing was fine for a day at the fair
and concert, not trying to make a good impression
on family and going to mass.

As always, it was as if he had read my mind.
He looked at me confidently and said, "Don't
worry, you look fine."

"Oh, thanks! 'Fine!' Why not just give me
the kiss of death?" I couldn't conceive how he
thought I looked good enough to meet anyone,
much less his mother.

"Don't worry, will you? Everyone is going

to like you as much as I do." He looked at me like he was trying to understand why this meant so much to me. He shook his head and turned his attention back to the road. The closer we got to his house, the more excited he got. He started pointing out places and telling me anecdotes about each.

I will never forget when he pointed to a restaurant and said, "There's the greasy spoon, oops! I mean the town diner." I had to laugh; his excitement was contagious.

My laughter died as we turned a corner and he pointed out his house. Then he named off who all the cars in the driveway belonged to: every member of his family. I felt like I was going to throw up.

"You planned this," I said, turning an accusing terrified frown on him as we stopped in front of the house. "I know you well enough now to know when I've been set up. So that's why you wanted to come down here so badly."

He started laughing so I hard I thought he was going to fall out of the truck. "I came down here to drop off the jet-ski and get cleaned up, just like I said. Honestly, I didn't know the whole family would be here."

I gritted my teeth and hung on to his hand like a lifeline as we entered the house. I immediately realized I didn't need the smile I had pasted on my face. This house seemed to radiate friendliness. He introduced me to everyone and we exchanged the usual pleasantries. But these weren't forced, I was truly pleased to meet them. His mother gave me such a welcoming smile I felt at ease. She gave him a hug and he hugged everyone after the introduction. Now I realized why his eyes always lit up when he talked about his home. This family loved each other, and I felt pulled into it.

I took the seat offered me and the house erupted in conversation with everyone all talking at once. I chatted with one brother about stereos. I wasn't very fluent in the language, but I had played a few very loudly in my time. I felt a hand on my shoulder and looked up to his handsome face. I never realized how little I knew about this man who just the night before had begged me not to cry. I was seeing a completely different side to him, another facet to this diamond-in-the-rough, if you will. It was one I was looking forward to seeing more of.

He heard the last of my conversation with his brother and asked if I would like to see his Mr. Stereo. I followed him upstairs to his room. To all of you reading this whose sudden intake of breath I just heard, the door was open the whole time. In fact, the one time I moved it so I could get by, his room was very crowded, he almost jumped over me to open it up again after I walked by.

He had an impressive stereo. I have no clue what kind it was, but the speakers were monstrous! He showed me a few other things before we went downstairs. He took great pride in his college diploma. He had worked very hard for that and it showed on his face. He told me the story about when he went to his younger brother's graduation. He said no one in his high school thought he would amount to much. When teachers asked him what he was doing lately, he loved the look on their faces when he told them he had just graduated from college and was working for a prominent firm nearby. I never pictured him as the type of man who would gloat, but after hearing the circumstances, I don't blame him.

He showed me around the house, talking to each family member as they raced by getting ready for mass. He took me into the family room and showed me a picture of him taken a short while before then. I looked at the picture, then to him, then to the picture again. He looked like a completely different man.

"I told you I was once very fat." There he was gloating again. I couldn't think badly of him one bit. I would be proud of myself also if I had made such a total turn-around in my life.

We left for mass before everyone else, therefore, we were the first to arrive. We walked up the middle aisle and took a seat. I had finished my prayers and was about to sit back when I heard a voice at my shoulder asking if they could sit there. I looked up and saw his whole family waiting in line to sit, with his mother in the lead. We slid down and mass started. I was so nervous with his mother sitting next to me, I actually forgot the prayers I had known for years. Speaking of praying, the only thing I prayed for was to get through this with as little embarrassment as possible. My hands were shaking so badly I couldn't hold the book we were reading from.

He noticed this and, when we were seated again for the Homily, he held his hand out for me to hold. I grabbed it and held onto it with a death grip until the point came in mass to exchange peace. I turned to him and shook his hand, then turned towards his mother. She gave me a hug and a kiss on the cheek before she did the same for him. To say I was surprised would be an understatement.

While the rest of the congregation was doing the same, I turned to him and joked, "Sure, your mother gives me a kiss, but from you I get a handshake." He smiled like that was his intention all along and bent down to give me a kiss before the father resumed mass.

I couldn't have walked out of that church happier. He stopped to say hello to a few people he knew and introduced me. Introducing me as his girlfriend, by the way. Nothing else about leaving mattered, except that he drove around and showed me where the older chapel was and few more 'monuments'. We were both so overwhelmingly happy, giddy is the only adjective that fits.

We arrived back at his house, but everyone

else was already there. He was still laughing about the joke he made. He had pulled into the school to show me where his classes were, or rather the windows of his classes, and as he did he said, "Watch, no cops."

I just looked at him wryly and this time shook my head. When we arrived, he took me by the hand and showed me around the outside of the house. He unloaded the jet-ski, we said goodbye to his family and left. We stopped at a gas station so he could fill his truck with gas and, as he waited, he knocked on my window. I rolled it down and he stuck his head in and grabbed a kiss.

"What was that for?" I laughed, surprised by his outlandish action.

He gave me my look and said, "Just 'cause I wanted to. I seem to remember someone saying I didn't need a reason to kiss her. Is she changing her mind?" he asked, raising an eyebrow.

"No, she isn't. Do it again!"

"Sorry, only one per customer," he laughed. I rolled the window up so I wouldn't hear him laughing at me. It didn't work, I saw him in the mirror loving this. By the time he got back in the truck though, he had managed to calm himself. For the first time I noticed how he actually got into the truck. He had to practically fold himself in half and duck his head to get in and out.

The drive to the fair was unbelievable. He took great pleasure in picking on me. Not a mean picking, but teasing just enough to make me laugh and even blush a couple times. I knew then that he was at ease with himself and me. To be perfectly honest, some of the time he was making a bigger fool of himself than me.

We parked where directed and he joked that it was up to me to remember where we were. He told me to lock my door, then came around to my side to 'check it' he said. By the way he looked at me I knew he wanted to ask me something, but couldn't find the words. This was the most handsome, intelligent, sensitive, and complicated man I had ever known; and he was driving me crazy! I told myself I should be happy he took his time to think out every word because, when it did come out, the words were so perfect and just what I wanted to hear, I couldn't be upset it took so long. My mother was always saying, 'If you're going to do something, you might as well do it right.'

We filled the day with the usual things one would do at the fair. We were looking at a display one jewelry vendor had, midway through the afternoon, and I saw two necklaces that I knew fit us perfectly. One was a heart with a key cut out and the other was the key. On the heart was written 'He who holds the key, holds my heart'. I pointed them out to him and he looked them over. He commented they were very nice, but continued looking over the rest of the case. When we moved on to another display, I figured my hint had fallen on deaf ears and focused on the new display.

We were on the other side of the fair when he stopped suddenly and looked at me, "So, is there anything you saw that you liked?"

"Yes, there is. I showed them to you in that jeweler's case." I was still keeping my promise to myself from the very beginning that I would be honest with him no matter what.

He grabbed my hand and started walking again. A few steps away he stopped again, "But are you ready for something like that?"

"I wouldn't have said so if I didn't think so,"

I returned. I had no idea what was going through his mind. Hadn't I just told him last night I was sure?

He turned us around and headed back for the jeweler's. When he had paid for them, the jeweler handed the bag over and I reached for it. He held it out of my reach and asked, "What do you think you're doing?"

"I was going to put it on," I answered innocently. He looked at me with such an expression of anger. I searched back over our conversation to see if I had said anything this offensive. I had never seen him mad; and if this was any indication of his temper, I *never* wanted to again.

"I bought the damn things. I'll give them to you when I'm good and ready," he snapped and started walking away. I was so stunned I stood there frozen to that spot. I still wasn't sure what I had done, but I wanted to make sure I never did it again. 'Oh, nuts,' I thought. 'Maybe he isn't ready. It's one thing to be together, but this would actually state it out-right. I did kind of push him into this. He, or we actually, are trying to learn to deal with our feelings realistically and now I go and make him do something he wasn't ready for. You moron! How would you like it if he pushed something onto you that you didn't really want? You would be damn mad, too!'

I was so busy berating myself that I didn't notice him stop and turn to see if I was following him. The look on his face made me want to turn and run. He held out his hand and, rather than running, I walked up to him, grabbed it, and tried to keep walking.

He squeezed my hand so hard to get my attention I had no choice but to stop. He put one finger under my chin and lifted my face up to his.

"I'm sorry I snapped," he started, but I quickly cut him off.

"No, I'm sorry. I had no right to assume. Can we just forget the whole thing and try to enjoy what is left of the day?" All I wanted to do was turn back time and never mention the things when he asked me that question again. That wasn't an impossible thing to ask, was it?

"Listen," he said more gently this time. He tipped my head up to him again. "Don't worry.

You'll get them, but *I* want to give it to you and *I* want to hang it around your neck.

Just...not...here." He spaced his last words far apart for the maximum effect and finished with a kiss. I wanted to insist that I was the one in the wrong and he had nothing to be forgiven for. I decided to leave well enough alone as I stared into his face.

We started towards the bandstand as it became time for the concert to start. We were next in line at the gate when he told me not to forget to remind him about something he wanted to ask me. I thought that was something I could manage without messing up too much. We found our seats and, before we could sit down, I heard familiar voices.

We had missed our meeting with my friend earlier in the day, so I was pleasantly surprised to see them sitting directly behind us. It never occurred to me that we would be sitting near each other. We borrowed my friend's binoculars and watched the concert through them for a song. He made us all laugh when he said, "Hey! She looks just like her posters!" You could always count on him to make a joke.

During the concert he gave me the necklace. He had perfect timing. We were standing, swaying to a slow song when he pulled it out and slipped it around my neck. He kissed the back of my neck when he finished latching it and shivers ran down my spine. I took out the key that matched my heart and hooked it behind his neck, kissing him the same way he did me, returning the shiver. Rather than letting me sit back in my seat, he pulled me onto his lap and kissed me thoroughly. The rest of the concert was a blur because we mostly necked through it. We came to our senses as the crowd stood up to applaud at the end.

Walking back to the truck, we bumped into his family walking to their car. We talked for a minute then we were walking to his truck again.

He unlocked my door, but wouldn't let me in. "Do you remember that question I wanted to ask you?" After I nodded, he continued, "Well, two very close friends of mine are getting married and I'm going to be in the wedding. That's not what I wanted to ask you. On the RSVP, there is a spot that says 'How many will be coming'. I wanted to know if I should put one or two?" I must have had a confused look on my face because he said, "Would you go with me?"

I had to steady myself or I would have floated away. The mistakes I had made that day just slipped into oblivion and I accepted with a nod of my head. That must not have been good enough for him, because he leaned forward and asked, "What was that?"

"Yes! Yes," I repeated and threw my arms around him and hugged him close.

He drove me back to my aunt's house and had to say a quick goodbye. He had to be at work at eight the next morning. I grabbed my suitcase and ran for the house. The only other thing I remember is touching the heart he gave me as one of the last things I did.

Chapter Six

I awoke the next morning and immediately started kicking myself for the things I did the day before. Like when you're having an argument with someone and can't think what to say; but the next day you ask yourself, 'Why didn't I say this?' or 'Why did I do that?' I ran the whole day over and over in my mind doing exactly that. I was so embarrassed about specific things that I blushed thinking about them. I actually smacked myself a few times thinking that would help. I became quite conscious of the fact that nothing would help now; what was done was done and making my arm sore wouldn't change anything.

The week went by in its usual routine: breakfast for the children, play, lunch for the children, play, supper for the children, play. It wasn't as droll as I make it sound, but I remember that week being simply one day after another. One day after another without a letter from him.

The only thing I had to look forward to was the mail coming. By the end of the week I didn't see any sense in rushing to the mailbox anymore. I had written him a letter and mailed it on Thursday so it would be there when he got home that week. I had taken up his style of writing a little every day like a diary. I also kept my personal diary at the same time. I did a lot of daily writing at one point in my life.

This week I didn't see any sense in continuing because, after the last weekend, he would never want to see me again, having given me the necklace or not. By Thursday afternoon I had taken my letter out of the mailbox three times and then put it back. I couldn't seem to get over the feeling that I couldn't fix whatever damage my mouth had managed to get me into. Again!

I suppose by now you are wondering just exactly what I said that was so bad. Other than the fiasco with the necklaces, I had to open the subject of my age with his family, I didn't mention it at the time I was telling the story because I didn't think it was important. But in order for you to understand the torment I was putting myself through, I think you should know.

This happened after mass. We had returned to his house and everyone was making preparations to go to the fair. He had gone upstairs after insisting I try a piece of his aunt's bread. I was eating very slowly, so as not to make a mess of crumbs on the table, and talking to his older sister. After everyone had decided which cars to take to the fair; they were out rearranging them in the driveway. One of his brothers let his sister drive his car out of the driveway and everyone was surprised she had even gotten it moving. I wondered what the fuss was about and she admitted to me she had never driven before or even had her permit. I was proud of the fact that I had passed the test for my permit on the first try, a minor accomplishment to be sure. I thought that would be a good way to impress her. After I informed her of the fact that I had just gotten my permit a week earlier, she almost dropped what she had just taken out of the microwave. The look in her eyes was a cross between 'How old are you anyways?' and 'If you are as old as you look, you must be pretty stupid to have just gotten your permit'.

I saw my mistake immediately, mumbled something about seeing her at the fair, and ran for the door. I bumped into him as he was walking into the house to get me. I looked up and quickly back down again. A glimpse was all it took to tell me he disapproved. Not disapproved really, but now was his turn to want to run. He wasn't hiding the fact that I was younger, but I'm pretty sure that was the *one* question he was not ready to discuss with anyone yet. It taught me a lesson, though. Even though you feel comfortable, never totally relax to the point you can't watch what you say.

When Friday came and there was still no letter, I gave up all hope. I just had to face the fact that I would never see him again. My uncle, aunt, and I were sitting at the table after supper, the children having already finished and playing, talking about one of my aunt's patients. I was actually moping.

My uncle saw this and was trying to cheer me up. He kept teasing me about how many stamps they had been going through lately. I didn't need cheering up, I needed a hug. But the one man who could do it was miles away by now.

I looked up from my soda and saw a truck pulling into the driveway. It didn't hit me for a minute whose it was until the driver reached above the visor to put his keys away. There was only one person I knew who did that.

I yelled, "It's him!" and raced from the house. My uncle made quick grab for the chair I was sitting in to keep it from toppling over.

I jumped down all six porch steps in my hurry to get out of the house. He had heard me scream from inside the house. He quickly shut the door of his truck and caught me as I hurled myself into his arms. He picked me up and swung me around in a big circle, laughing blissfully. We kissed after he set me down and we stood there holding one another making up for the past week

"I take it you didn't get my letter," he laughed. We started walking back in the direction I had just come from, this time taking our time with our arms around each other.

"No, I didn't get your letter. You mean you wrote me after last weekend?" I asked. To me, at that moment in time, it sounded ridiculous.

"Yes, I wrote you," he said with obvious disbelief. "You really didn't get it?"

"No," I answered. What a load off my mind. He had written after all. He wasn't ashamed of me. Most importantly, he came to see me and wasn't miles away like I thought. He was here and he was with me, all else seemed insignificant.

We walked in to find my aunt and uncle looking at us like we were crazy. My uncle told him that, if he was going to visit, he should let us know so I didn't break anymore chairs. We all had a big laugh over that. I couldn't hear most of the conversation because I was busy with my own thoughts. I wasn't thinking at all, but only feeling. I gave his hand a little squeeze and he looked at me with a look of intense serenity. He was so comfortable, sitting there. Like there was no other place in the world he would rather be and nothing he would rather be doing than holding my hand and looking at me.

My older cousin picked right then to come barreling in from the living room and jumped him from behind. He untangled himself from my cousin's arms and dropped him on the floor. That was the sign he was looking for. He stood up and announced that it looked like the sun was going down.

He looked at me with those eyes and asked if I would like to see the sun set from the beach. I looked at my aunt and held my breath, hoping she would approve. She nodded her head and smiled. I was right. She wasn't stupid. She knew exactly what was going on. My uncle said something about driving safely as we walked out the door, but neither of us really heard him.

I couldn't believe my luck. Not thirty minutes before I had been feeling sorry for myself because I had lost something very close to me; and now I was seated next to him in his truck going to watch the sunset. It was incredibly romantic. I wasn't to know how romantic until we reached the beach.

We parked the truck by the pier and sat there for a minute. A cabin-cruiser was going by and he commented how he would like to own a boat like that someday. He said he wanted to buy another jet-ski and tie both of them to the back so he could take off cruising whenever he wanted to. He was talking about the future and testing the waters, so to speak. I mentioned 'his and hers' jet skis, testing the water a little myself, and he just laughed.

"Yeah, I think my little sister would like one," he joked. I couldn't help laughing. He knew exactly what I was talking about; he just wanted to see if he could throw in a joke. Next he mentioned buying a house. I was quite taken aback. Buying a house was a big step, and I told him so.

"Well, it's getting to the point in my life when I have to start planning a future. I'm going to be married someday and I'd like to be able to come home like a normal person. You know, 'Honey, I'm home' and all that jazz."

"And have kids scream 'Daddy's home!' Yeah, I know what you mean. I never thought of you as a homebody. I always pictured you as a party animal," I laughed, thinking he was still kidding around. He wasn't though, and the tone in his voice told me that.

"Well, recent events caused me to take a good look at my life and re-evaluated my priorities. One of my friends is already married and one more is about to. It makes a person think."

"I know. It makes a person think long and hard, but keeping up with your friends is no reason to rush around to get things accomplished," I said. Just what was he getting at? Is this the same man who less than a week before thought he was too young to be tied down? The way he was talking and the way I was feeling, one would not think twice about the direction of this conversation. But I had learned the hard way not to jump to any conclusions.

He abruptly jumped in his seat like someone had stuck him with a pin. "I promised you a sunset, didn't I? Well, I happen to know that there is one right over there," he said, pointing to the beach.

He was right. The sun was just above the horizon and quickly falling from view. He led me to a part of the beach that was grassy, rather than sandy, and sat me down. We sat there on the beach holding each other, our attention on the sun.

It really was blinding. It fell behind a small cloud and its intensity shattered the sky. Before the last arc disappeared below the horizon, it exploded into a fantastic light display. One of the last remaining beams reached across the miles and engulfed my heart.

Earlier, we had been throwing stones at the spiders building webs between the rocks at the edge of the water. With one quick motion, he threw the remaining rocks in his hand into the water and turned towards me. He looked at me, then back at the last light of the sun, then back to me, trying to find the strength to start saying what he wanted to say. He turned back to me one last time, a smile on his face now, and began his confession.

"You know," he began, looking out over the lake again, "that I have never said 'I love you' to anyone. So I thought, while I was up here, I would tell someone."

He looked back at me with such power in his completely unmasked eyes that I couldn't face him. I tried to look down and focus my attention on the spiders.

"Now, you've got to look at me when I say this," he said as he reached over to tilt my head up to his. "I love you."

He said it so slowly and surely that my breath stuck deeper and deeper in my throat with each word. He was looking at me as if his very life depended upon my reaction.

I had been in love with him since the day we spent together at the beach. I didn't want to relive the helpless feeling of the catch-22 I had been caught up in the night before the fair. He knew I didn't take this emotion lightly, as neither did he. Would he take me seriously? Did I take the time to explain? 'No," I told myself, 'this is where you close your eyes and take a leap of faith.'

"I know that because I'm sixteen, people may think I don't know the meaning of love. This is the strongest, most powerful, long-lasting kind of love there is. And I mean it when I say I love you."

This time I was the one whose life depended upon his reaction. He pulled me into his arms and said he understood what I meant.

I pulled back just far enough to be able to look into his eyes. "You know, now that you've got me, you'll have a hell of a time getting rid of me," I laughed.

"You won't have to worry about that," he said and pulled me back into his arms. At that moment I knew this was where I was meant to be. Wrapped up in his embrace and totally encircled by his love.

We spent the rest of the evening walking around and glowing. We had no particular destination in mind. We walked by the same ride at least twenty times. I made a mention if his family knew where he was, remembering the call we made at the state park. He laughed and said they would figure it out. If his mom started to worry his dad would tell her he stopped to see his girl. He shook his head at his dad understanding how he felt.

He said the sweetest thing, which rapidly became one of his trademarks, like 'my' look. He would look at me and say, "Well, now that we are *in love*, what would you like to do now?" His eyes told me the whole story. I had heard of eyes dancing with happiness, but that doesn't completely describe what I saw in them. Pride, relief, love, happiness, contentment all seemed to take up residence there. My heart felt like bursting. I didn't think I had a big enough heart to hold all the love I felt for him, and now that I knew he loved me too, it swelled even more.

I asked him what his family thought of me. He paused and started laughing. He said there was a funny story attached to that question.

"Well, tell me. Don't just leave me in suspense." I told him. He led me to a bench and we sat down. He stretched his legs out in front of him and put his arm around me.

"I told you I had already told my little sister about you, but when I got home Monday, Mom wanted to know all about you. The first thing she asked was how old you are. She was surprised to hear you are only sixteen, but she seemed to accept it." He was sitting there with his arm around me, drawing little circles on my shoulder, like it was the most natural thing in the world, while I was hanging on his every word.

"What? Do you mean she accepted it? Did she like me? You don't know surprised I was when she hugged me at mass last week."

"She knew you were young, but I don't think she was prepared for just how young. She knows how I feel about you, so she didn't say anything. Yes, she liked you. She said you seemed like a very nice girl. I asked her why she gave you a hug during mass, myself. She said it didn't seem right to her that she was hugging all her children and not you. By the way, she noticed how nervous you were. We both had a laugh about you thinking I had planned the whole thing." He started laughing again just remembering the look on my face when I realized I would be meeting his entire family. I started laughing with him. It must have been comical watching me shake hands with everyone with this horrified look on my face.

I picked out the one word from his story that didn't seem to fit. "Nervous? I was nervous? My hands were shaking so bad I couldn't hold the book steady. I wasn't nervous at all. I was terrified!" I had leaned forward and turned towards him at the beginning of my speech and pointed my finger at him emphasizing every word.

"All right, all right," he soothed me, pulling me back against him. "I noticed you were shaking, that's why I held out my hand. I figured you needed some strength and could draw from mine." He paused for a minute, then added, "Boy, that sounds corny." He started shaking his head as if he couldn't believe what he just said.

I reached over with my hand and turned his face towards mine, loving the feeling that he had done this so many times to me, now I had the opportunity to do it for him. "It's not corny at all. It was just what I needed. It seems like you read my mind at times. You either seem to say or write exactly what I need to hear. That's one of the things I love about you."

I said it so sincerely; I don't think he was prepared. He looked at me in wonder and said, "That's right. You do, don't you?" We kissed until we both noticed the people going by giving us funny looks. Why was it so easy to forget everything but each other?

"Let's find a place a little less public," he said and took my hand to lead me back to where the truck was parked. Before he unlocked my door, ever the gentleman, he said the words that are burned into my heart forever. "Do you remember what you said about having a hard time getting rid of you? Well, I feel the same way. You will have a hard time getting rid of me, too." He opened the door and we headed in the direction of my house.

About halfway home, he took a quick glance at me and dropped another unexpected confession on me. "There was one thing everyone said about you," he started as he chanced another look at me. "I'm not saying you're not pretty, but, everyone thought I would bring home a knock-out, a real bomb-shell."

I have to say, I was stunned. I never thought

my looks would come under such close scrutiny. I was dressed for a day at the fair. My immediate reaction was to be offended. "Well, I'm sorry if I disappointed them!" I snapped.

We pulled into the driveway in silence. He sat staring straight in front of him and I was waiting for his response. "Listen, I never should have told you." He was still staring straight ahead out the windshield. "You didn't disappoint anybody. They all liked you." He turned towards me to finish. "I think you're beautiful, and I am the only one who matters. *I* love you."

"I love you, too. I guess I overreacted. I just never expected you to be totally honest about that. I want you to be honest, but – oh hell!" I finished. I knew I was burying myself deeper with every word, so decided to shut up.

He just shook his head and leaned forward to kiss me. We went inside to visit with my aunt and uncle. It was a pleasant evening, but it was hard to sit there and talk calmly when we were in love and wanted to be alone. Finally, he said his goodbyes and I told my aunt I was going to walk him out to his truck. We giggled all the way out and burst when we made it off the porch. Nothing was funny, we were so exhilarated to be together laughing was a reasonable outlet.

We held each other by the truck, neither of us wanting to let go and we started talking. Somehow we ended up in his truck until two in the morning. We talked for three hours and it seemed like five minutes. He looked at me with my look and repeated how amazing it was that he could tell me anything.

Yep, again, we managed to fog up his windows. I remember writing 'I love you' on the passenger side of his windshield. He reached over and wrote 'and you too' underneath. It was such a silly little thing, but I wanted him to have something to think about when he drove home. Every time he made a right turn, he saw it. He told me later that he wouldn't let his sister wash that part of the window and erase it. It's curious how little things end up being the most romantic memories.

Chapter Seven

I received his letter the next day. Even though he had already told me everything in it, I still raced to the mailbox to get it. I told him in my letter that Tuesday we would have known each other for one month. In his letter, he said we should consider Friday as one month, because that was when he met the real me. As touching as that sentiment was, it felt foreign to me to measure what we had in time increments. One month did not equal how much we knew about each other or what we had shared and learned. What is one month in time when it felt like you've known another person forever?

We had talked about how we would manage to see each other when I moved back home with my mother to start the school year. It was another hour drive from his house. I suggested he stop on his way home from work, that way saving him some driving time and having another reason to look forward to weekends. He thought that was a good idea. He kept repeating that the following Monday was a paid holiday, hinting at something I suspect. I didn't want to discourage him from seeing me, but

I wanted to give my mother a chance to get used to the idea of me having a boyfriend. Most importantly, *I* wanted to be the one to explain our age difference to her.

As you have gathered by now, my mother was extremely old-fashioned in her thinking. She and my father divorced before I started kindergarten and I visited him on weekends and vacations. I was to have spent the summer with him that year. When my grandmother fell ill and my aunt asked it I wanted to help with her children, I had originally thought my summer had taken a turn for the worse. If only I had known.

Anyways, my mother raised the youngest of seven children by herself. I'm not saying this to gain your sympathy; I want you to know why she was so strict. Maybe strict isn't the word, but she had certain convictions that could not be shaken with any amount of pleading.

When my mother remarried a man with eight children, I then became the youngest of fifteen. Take a moment to absorb that number. I made out like a bandit on Christmas and birthdays, but, when it came to getting away with anything, she and my new dad had plenty of practice dealing with it. I should have made a recording of her favorite line so she could play it back to me at least once a week. 'None of your brothers or sisters did, it wouldn't be fair for you to.'

One of my mother's rules was no 'dating' until I was sixteen. I went to a couple of school dances, movies, and had calls from boys, but that was it. I simply wasn't interested in any of the boys I was friendly with in school. I was smarter than most of them, and more mature than all of them. I think I offended one poor boy when he was trying to kiss me at a dance and I burst out laughing. I never had any interest in bringing anyone home for her approval. What was the sense of her meeting someone I didn't care if she liked or not?

This wasn't the problem with him. He was a well-brought-up, all-American male, who was stable and respectable, and went to mass. 'What's not to like?' I asked myself. His age would matter to her. I only prayed she would like him for his personality and not immediately dislike him because he was eight years older. Unexpectedly I realized I may be giving my mother too little credit.

She had always taught me not to 'judge a book by its cover'. And she was the type of person to practice what she preached. When I came to that conclusion, I decided there was nothing to worry about. I was nervous, or maybe it was excitement, but not scared anymore. I wanted her to get to know the man who meant so much to me, but I wasn't going to make myself sick with worry over it. She would make her own decision without my influencing her.

My father picked me up at my aunt's to take me back to my mother's later that weekend. In the car, I was reading his letter one last time before I had to concentrate on the upcoming school year when I opened the window. Before I could stop it, a page of the letter flew out the window and landed in the road behind us. My father cracked up laughing when I told him what happened! At least he turned around so I could retrieve it off the road. My hands were shaking when I picked it up; I had come so close to losing one of the few things I had to hold onto when he wasn't there to hold himself. I told my father about him on the way home. He said he sounded nice enough.

When we reached my mom's house, I gave Dad a kiss goodbye and bolted for the house. I had laid out my strategy to tell my mother about my boyfriend, but as I was to find out, she already knew. One of my other aunt's had told my dad, who told my sister, who told my mother. Needless to say, she was full of questions about him. And, just as anticipated, the first question was 'how old is he?' Apparently, the grapevine hadn't said his age, just that he was older.

She didn't explode the way I thought she would. Here I was prepared for World War III, and she just exhaled in an exaggerated sigh.

"Boy, you sure didn't waste any time. You just turned sixteen and you're already going steady," she said.

"I didn't plan it this way, Mom," I said out loud, but thought to myself, 'I don't think I could have planned meeting the man of my dreams on a camping trip.'

I continued, "And I wouldn't call it going steady," trying to avoid any more questions. I knew no answer I could give her would be good enough.

"If you wouldn't call it going steady, then what's this?" she asked, picking up the heart off my t-shirt. Did she have to scrutinize everything?

"He gave me that at the fair," I deflected, turning away.

"I think you did plan this," she laughed. "I wish I had a nickel for every time you said, 'I can't wait until I'm sixteen.'"

I laughed too. We would have been millionaires by then, that was my favorite comeback at one point. She asked me how often I saw him. She was noticeably surprised when I told her every weekend but one, so far.

"So, it's pretty serious," she said quietly. She looked at me with a lost look in her eyes that said, 'You're on your own now; I just hope you don't get hurt.'

'I hope so, too!' I answered her in my thoughts. She asked me a couple more questions about him, mostly where we went and what we did. I tried my best to deflect her questions. Now I know how he felt when he had been questioned by his mother after the fair. I was having a difficult time trying to explain to her things I couldn't explain to myself: things I simply knew and felt. This was the first time I had an actual conversation with my mother, as a person. Normal conversations would be like this: Mom, Can I? NO! She seemed anxious to know if I had kept my curfew and then relieved to know I had.

"What does he think about you having to be in by eleven?"

"It's never actually come up," I answered honestly. "In most cases, it's a good thing. He has a long drive home and is usually beat the next day."

I was very happy, and a little 'weirded-out' that we could talk this way. Did she notice the changes in me over the summer in the past few minutes? Of course she did, she was Mom. We had become friends, rather than disciplinarian and defensive child. She was honest about not liking the age difference, but she said she would have to meet him before she would make up her mind.

"I assume you will be seeing him next weekend, then. I will have to get to know him then," she said, dismissing the subject. I decided not to push any further and to take what little approval she gave as a good sign. I went to my room, unpacked, then wrote him a long letter trying to explain the astonishing discussion.

The next morning, when I asked for a stamp, her eyebrows went up in surprise. "You write him? Does he write you back?" I must have given her a strange look because she returned with her 'and don't give me a smart-aleck response' face. I tried to explain the delicate balance of long-distance relationships to her and she seemed to understand. Even today, I'm not completely sure she really did understand, but at least she gave me the stamp.

School started the next day. It was a normal first day: seating assignments, teachers handing out books, dodging seventh-graders who were looking scared and lost most of the time. I really felt sorry for them. I remember my first day in the big school. By now it was the same boring routine; but then, I walked around the whole day terrified.

When I got home, I had a letter from him. I walked in the house like every other ordinary time, but there, prominently displayed on the table, was his letter. And on the other side of the room was my mother, amazed he honestly did write.

It was a regular letter. He was bored with work and depressed. I chalked his depression up to it being Monday when he wrote the letter. I was worried, though, deep inside. The next day I decided to do something to try and cheer him up. I never thought that he might be in a better mood by the time I received his letter two days later; I had this sense of helplessness and needed to try.

I walked into town and bought him a couple of funny pins. Later that night I felt philosophical and decided to vent my frustration by writing. I scribbled a few things down, but nothing seemed to be working. 'I need a good laugh,' I thought, so I decided to try and write something light-hearted. I finished a truly terrible poem, dated it, then put it in with the pins in my letter to him. I mailed it the next day. I probably should have waited. He was planning to stop and see me on Friday, only two days away.

School filled the days and before I knew it, I was watching out the windows Friday afternoon.

It is truly ironic how the meeting I was fearing most, is the single one time we had together I remember least. I introduced him to Mom and they started talking. He made a comment about his little sister's new boyfriend. He was older than she was at the time.

My mother picked up on that right away. "That's like your age difference," she said, nodding to us.

He shifted in his seat and tried to cover by saying he had always been overprotective of her. I jumped in and changed the subject to anything but ages.

The next week couldn't have gone by any slower unless we had slowed the clocks. I didn't do any homework all week, saving it all to do on Friday night. I got a letter from him halfway through the week saying he would be up on Saturday. I was glad of that because we could spend the whole day together; but I was at a loss for ideas how to get through the rest of the week. He had written me a six page letter and gave it to me when he came the weekend before, so I decided to return the favor. I would write him a little everyday and in each class when my teachers thought I was taking notes.

I never took notes in school. I have a memory like a computer. I have always, even to this day, wanted to test it to see if it is really photographic or not.

I learned in elementary school how to remember by association. I could look back in my mind and picture the teacher telling us something. It amazed some teachers, and thoroughly annoyed others. The latter thought I should be taking notes of every word that came out of their mouths. I had one teacher who would try to trip me up by asking what she said at the very beginning of class if she found me looking out the window. I loved repeating word-for-word what she said and watching her eyes get that glow that meant she would love to send me to detention. One time she actually threatened me, "We'll see how you do on the test when you have no notes to study from."

I still, to this day, wish I could have seen the look on her face as she was grading my paper. I missed one question, but got the bonus question correct, ending up with a perfect score. I wasn't trying to egg her on or start trouble, I didn't think every word out of her mouth was as important as she did.

He used to love kidding me about my memory and putting himself down for his lack of one. I was always quick to reassure him that I didn't care what he forgot, as long as he remembered he loved me. That always brought a smile and a kiss.

To get back to what I was saying, by the end of the week, I had a twenty page letter for him. I didn't trust it going out with a single stamp, so a friend of mine walked over to the post office with me to get it weighed to send it out with absolutely correct postage. All the way there and back she kept bugging me about when she was going to meet him. 'Other friends had met him, why not her?' she kept asking. After a few non-committal replies, I finally had to give in just to get her off my back.

"He's coming up on Saturday. If he wants to, we will drive over and see you. O.K?" I didn't want to share any of my time with him with anyone else. I realized the flaw in my thinking. I was so happy he wanted to keep our relationship out in the open, now I wanted to do just the opposite. I made a mental note: Have him meet more friends…but not too many. They *all* have incriminating and embarrassing stories about you.

Chapter Eight

I woke up that Saturday morning later than I usually do. I had been up late the night before catching up on the work I had put off. I jumped in the shower and took my time doing the usual weekend chores. I wanted to make them last as long as possible to take up the time before he was to arrive. I closed myself in my room for an hour and a half just doing my hair and make-up. 'He met me at my worst,' I thought, 'let's show him our best.' There was something about this visit. I'd never claimed to be psychic, but I had a feeling about that day and wanted to look my best when he arrived.

A few minutes before two in the afternoon, he pulled into the driveway. That was one day when his timing was lousy. We had just finished lunch and I was up to my elbows in soapy water finishing the dishes. If I had my way, I would have run out to the truck and mugged him before he opened the door.

My mother had a different idea. "He knows the way into the house," she said. "Hurry and finish the dishes and maybe you will be done before he comes in."

Just then he knocked at the door. My father let him in, or rather motioned to him through the window in the door. My older brother was there. He had dropped by to ask my father's advice about something and, when he heard he was coming, decided to stay and snoop.

I apologized for the dishes, then introduced my brother. The look on my brother's face was precious. He was constantly putting down my boyfriends, as older brothers do. This time he could find nothing wrong. In fact, I think he was a little envious. My brother drove a beat-up truck and wasn't much into fashion. He thought this guy had it all together. He drove a new truck and, if I may say so, looked very nice.

After my brother left, Dad and he talked about engines for a while as I put the finishing touches on the kitchen. My father was fixing the lawn mower and had parts all over the garage. He noticed them on his way in and figured that was a ground they both had in common.

My mother showed him through the house as I was finding my other shoe in the disaster of my closet. I can't blame her for being proud of it. She and my father built the house themselves. It took almost three years to complete, but, with only two workers, the progress was slow. The only elements they didn't handle themselves were the electric, furnace installation, and pouring the cellar wall.

I didn't have to worry about him though. He seemed very relaxed as he chatted about engines and house stories. I rescued him just in time, though, as my father was about to launch into an embarrassing story about how I almost broke my ankle jumping in and out of the wall studs before the house was totally enclosed. Or did I rescue myself? I could tell by the way he was looking at me that he would much rather be alone with me than listening to that story as well.

As we were leaving, my mother asked us what our plans were. I looked at him and he just looked back blankly. "This is your town, what do you want to do?" he asked. I told him I promised to introduce him to a friend, but I didn't have anything planned.

Mom just looked at us like we were crazy. She reminded me about mass before I left and the idea dawned on me that I could have a kind of payback before the day was out. My plan was to have him sit next to my mother during this afternoon's mass like I sat next to his mother during the mass before the fair. He had had such a good time with the fact that I shook through the service, I wanted him to know what it felt like.

We hopped in his truck and drove away. It was as if the scene had replayed itself as I looked up in the house windows as we were leaving and saw my mother looking out, smiling that he had opened the door for me. We weren't even a mile away from the house when he abruptly pulled into a parking lot and put the truck in neutral.

"I have been waiting for this all day," he said and pulled me into his arms. I'm not sure how long we kissed, but it could have gone on for a lifetime for me.

He reluctantly put the truck in gear again. "So, where is this friend I'm supposed to meet?" he asked cheerily.

I pointed in the direction he should go, but remained silent. I was beginning to think this was a bad idea. I really didn't want these two to meet. My friend never seemed to think so, but she was beautiful. She had long, brown hair, soft skin and a body that never quit. I tried to tell her that she turned all the boys' heads when she walked by; but every time I would bring up the subject, she would turn it around and say they were looking at me. Now that was a ridiculous thought.

Every time we came to a turn, I would tell him which way to go, but nothing else. I was so absorbed in my thoughts.

"If you don't say something soon, I am going to pull this truck over and shake you," he said.

I looked at him, daring him to do it. He looked back just as determined. I didn't think he was serious until he turned his signal on and started to pull over.

"All right, all right," I laughed.

"Good. Now what is the matter?" He was gloating. I should have smacked him or something, but I just grabbed his hand and gave it a loving squeeze.

"Nothing is the matter," I answered, but his eyes told me he didn't believe me. "I feel funny about you meeting my friend." There, I said it, honesty always. I had it out in the open, and so help him if he laughed.

"What is it? Is she the knock-out I have been looking for?"

"Yes!" I shouted. That was it! I had reached the end of my worrying. I knew he was just kidding around, but I was so insecure after hearing the comment from his family that this was no longer a laughing matter.

"Look," he said, shaking his hands against the steering wheel to emphasize his words. "I have only said I love you to one girl in my life! Do you think I'm just going to forget that and run after one of her friends?"

He was right. I hadn't thought of this from his perspective. "And, if you think I would, you don't know me very well," he finished.

"I'm sorry. I didn't think of this from that point of view. I didn't mean to put you in a position to defend yourself. But she is a knock-out!"

"I don't care! If you've forgotten that you're the one I love already, I might have to remind you!" He had started the sentence with such a firm voice, I thought I had said the wrong thing to make him understand. But when he laughed as he said the last, I knew things would be all right.

We pulled into the driveway of her house shortly thereafter. He was still thinking about it though. We both were, and he gave me a reassuring kiss before we opened the door to go in.

It was just as I should have expected. She was fooling around in the kitchen and practically jumped on me when her mother showed us in. She didn't wait for an introduction. She just started talking as if she'd known him for years. She then proceeded to embarrass me by telling stories about the hi-jinx we had gotten into the year before. He looked at me amazed. This was definitely showing a side of me to him he had never seen before.

She ended by saying, "I'm glad to see her grown up and respectable. It was a tough job, but somebody had to do it. I'm sure not going to." She said the last as she snuck a bite of something from the frig. He and I both laughed.

I couldn't believe I had been worried about him finding her attractive. She was pretty, but when it came to brains or common sense, she was definitely lacking. A male 'friend' of hers came over and the four of us decided to drive back to town and get some ice-cream at the new parlor that had opened.

The drive there was a riot. He drove like a madman. Both men did. They drove ahead of us and kept speeding up and slowing down, then on the wrong side of the road until they hit a blind spot. That's the only way we knew there was a curve ahead. Once they could see, it was crazy time again. We laughed at them all the way to town.

Once they crossed the town line and met the speed limit, the obeyed every traffic law. He said something about wishing he was a cop sometimes, which only made me laugh harder. We parked in front of the ice-cream shop and waited for the others to get out of the car.

We all walked in together and let the screen door slam behind us. From somewhere in the shop we heard a pig oink. All four of us stared at the other shocked. My friend said something very loud and we heard it again. We finally tracked down the sound. There was a stuffed pig on the counter at one side of the shop. We all read the sign above it simultaneously and burst out laughing.

"Sonic Pig," we said together.

"It's activated by loud noises," the owner said. He had been standing behind the counter watching us and having a private laugh of his own.

We ordered and then sat down at a table near the pig. We then proceeded to make as much noise as possible to make the pig talk. My friend would pretend it talked back by making up words for its oinks.

"Oh, really? You've been sitting up there all day?" Oink, oink. "Your butt is sore? I bet it would be!" Oink, oink. We were all in the right frame of mind for that to be hilarious.

A couple of young kids came in and the screen door slammed behind them. Oink, oink

"Hey, that pig is talking to you," he said. He looked at me with my look and continued to irritate the kids. "Aren't you going to answer it?" he asked when they walked for the door. "How rude!" when they left.

I must have given him a look of disapproval because he looked back innocently and shrugged his shoulders. It was such an adorable 'little boy' reaction that I started laughing all over again.

We finished out ice-cream after having decided to leave the pig in peace. I couldn't believe the change in him. I would have thought we were in his hometown. He always seemed to draw energy from just talking about it. He was joking around with these two like he'd known them for years. I felt I had to do something, I couldn't sit still any longer. I leaned over and put my hand on his leg to steady myself and kissed him.

"What was that for?" he asked surprised.

"Do I need a reason?" I asked back with an innocent look of my own.

"No," he said, shaking his head. "Do it again."

And I did. My friend looked at me like I'd lost my mind. We kissed one more time and she reacted. She jumped up from her chair wiping her mouth with a napkin. "Ooo. Gross. Don't do that in front of me! Have some decency. Can't you see I'm trying to eat here?"

He took that as a challenge. He put his arm around me, pulled me close, and kissed me fervently. For the rest of time we stayed in the shop, every time we kissed, she would throw a fit.

Each time she did, I got another kiss. I was happily caught up in the wicked little circle those two had created.

We left the restaurant, after saying goodbye to the pig of course, and went our separate ways. We got back into his truck and he asked me where to go now. We decided to drive around because we wanted to get back to my house for mass by a little after four.

"That's what I wanted to do today!" He said suddenly. We were sitting in the parking lot we had just turned around in, waiting for traffic to clear. "I wanted to teach you how to drive this thing," he finished, patting the dashboard.

"No way!" I exclaimed. I was horrified at the thought. I did such a good job of making a fool of myself already today, I didn't need a driving lesson to help me. Besides, I had seen his temper before and didn't want to chance wrecking his truck.

"What do you mean, 'No way'?"

"Ahh, I don't have my permit with me," I lied. I couldn't think of a good reason that he wouldn't simply dismiss.

"That's a pretty lame excuse," he countered. "If you don't want to, just say so."

"I don't want to," I said, deliberately. He started shaking his head and I knew what that meant. "I don't want you to get mad and holler at me if I broke something," I explained.

"I don't holler when I get mad—" he started.

"You lie!" I interrupted. "I've talked to your sister. Remember?"

"Well, if she would stop wearing my clothes, I wouldn't have to. Besides, I don't get mad, I get even," he grinned, trying to sound menacing. It didn't work.

"Remind me never to get you mad at me," I laughed.

"You know what they say: It's the pay back that's the bitch," he laughed back.

We drove around and I pointed out the few 'monuments' in my town as he had done in his. We made it back to my house just in time; my parents were just getting ready for church.

Inside he said, "So, you're really going to make me go, aren't you?" He was looking at me with a contemplative look on his face.

"You don't have to go," my mother put in. "I don't think it will hurt you, though."

He looked quickly at my mother, then back to me. "I know it won't hurt me, but I know she has something up her sleeve."

I giggled evilly and ran into my room to check my appearance. I wasn't concerned with my looks, I had used enough hairspray that morning that my hair wouldn't move for a week. I wanted to get away from his probing eyes. All day he had been looking at me oddly. I would turn around and find him studying me. I would always smile, but he would have this strange look on his face that made me excited and wary at the same tine.

He had had that look on his face when I left the room, but when I entered again, he looked at me like I had been gone for days. I saw the love in his eyes and couldn't wait for church services to be over so we could be alone again. Just his touch would send my heart spinning and I wanted to feel more.

We drove to church separately and waved to them as we drove past to park closer than they did. When we entered, I could feel his grip change as it was holding my hand. He finally figured out what I had up my sleeve. We sat first and my mother asked if we could move down so they could sit by the aisle.

Halfway through mass, I felt he had sweated enough and held out my hand. He grabbed it and squeezed it to say, "You're going to pay for this!"

Seeing us holding hands, my mother gave me a look of approval. When it came time to exchange peace; we kissed before he turned to my mother. She stretched her arms up and gave him a hug. I looked at her amazed. She had just hugged my boyfriend in front of God and everyone we knew and then shook hands with the people around her like this was an every day occurrence. If that wasn't a stamp of approval, I don't know what was. And, just like it set my fears aside when his mother hugged me, he seemed more relaxed and enjoyed the rest of the service.

After mass was over, we ran for the truck, hand in hand. He pulled me into his arms before he opened the door for me. "You had the whole thing planned, didn't you?" he asked.

I got into the truck before I answered, "The

thought didn't really hit me until my mother mentioned it before we left for my friend's house. Somebody said, 'I don't get mad, I get even!'"

"Leave it to you to turn my own words against me," he laughed.

"You weren't really nervous, were you?" I was having a hard time believing he was intimidated by anything.

"Nervous? I was scared to death!" he laughed. "It was just as if the situation was reversed." He looked back at the church and shook his head before he started the engine.

"So, where to next?" he asked.

"I don't know. You're the boss. Where do you want to go?"

"Oh, now I'm the boss, am I?" he asked with eyebrows raised. "I am nowhere near the boss," he said very seriously.

I didn't pick up n the tone in his voice. I continued in a lighthearted was. "Well, I'm sure not the boss!"

He turned to me with a sad look on his face. "Does anyone have to be the boss?"

"No, no" I said, realizing I had missed

something somewhere.

Back at the house, he saw my brother and sister-in-law working with a cow next door. My brother took over the family farm when my father retired. My parents had built their house down the road and the barnyard and our lawn bordered each other.

When he turned off the truck, he said hello to my brother again. I asked if there was a problem with the cow. My brother said she was just having twins and he wanted to be there in case anything happened.

We went into the house after I introduced my sister-in-law to him. My mother looked at the clock, then looked at us, then back to the clock again. "So, where have you been? Mass ended almost thirty minutes ago."

I could have died right then and there. I was so embarrassed. Now we had to check in? The mortified look on my face was enough to tell her that comment was out-of-line.

He took the question in stride, though, and

told her we were just talking about getting even. That opened the flood gates. By the time we had told her the whole story about the mass before the fair, she was almost in tears with laughter.

"Sure, Mom, laugh at the most humiliating moment of my life," I said sarcastically.

"But that's what makes it so funny," she said and kissed my cheek.

"And you can stop laughing any time!" I said to him. He tried desperately to stop, but the look on my face when I said that just set him off again.

My father came out of the bedroom after changing his clothes and noticed my brother and the cow through the window.

"Ever seen twins born before?" he asked him. "Now's your chance."

I never thought twice about my actions or what repercussions they would have later, but I jumped up, grabbed his hand and headed for the door. I didn't know what I intended to accomplish, but I wanted to do something for him. When I thought about it later that night, I realized what a really stupid thing it was to do. But when he told my father he hadn't seen anything born, I thought I could do something that no one had done for him. That was what I was thinking as we watched the birth. I was giving him something nobody else ever could.

After the calves were taken care of, he and my brother started talking about school. They had gone to the same college but at different times. The cows in the barn were causing quite a racket, signaling milking time, so we headed back inside the house.

Mom asked us if we were staying for diner so she knew how many hot dogs to cook. It had been a long standing tradition that on Saturday night we always had hot dogs for supper. When or how that started, no one knows. But it certainly wasn't my idea of a romantic ending to a perfect day.

Apparently, it wasn't his either. He thanked her but declined, "I've got to check out the restaurants around here."

"They don't cook things any different up here than they do where you live," She stated.

I rolled my eyes heavenward and prayed, 'Take a hint, Mom' when she turned back to the stove.

He looked at me and asked, "Where would you like to go?"

"I'm not sure. What are you in the mood for?" I asked back.

"Hey, it's your town. You know the places better than I do."

"I don't know all of them," I said. Neither of us wanted to make a decision. It could have gone on for hours, but something he was saying triggered a response from my mother.

"You're the boss," he said, smiling that he could use my words against me this time.

"You mean you let her make decisions? Oh Boy, are you in trouble now," my mother laughed. She had turned away from the stove and was waving the fork she was turning hot dogs with at me.

"MO-om," I whined, once again mortified.

"Wha-at," she whined back, mimicking my tone and expression.

He viewed all this with a look on his face like he had watched this scene hundreds of times before. He did have a mother and younger sister at home. He came over, grabbed my shoulders and steered me towards the door.

"Come on," he laughed. "We better get you out of here before your mother stabs you with that fork."

She made a brandishing motion with the fork and we ran for the door. After finally deciding on a restaurant, I gave him directions and we were off.

Diner was a fun affair. He teased me about the way I fixed my salad. I can still see the look on his face when the waitress asked me if I wanted anything from the bar, then asked him for proof of age before she would bring his drink. He couldn't believe he was being carded. He told her to forget the drink and just bring him a soda when she brought mine. He looked at me with an evil look and took a minute to put his words together for maximum effect.

"You enjoyed that, didn't you?" he asked. The effect he wanted, he didn't get. The combined look on his face with the obviously dangerous tone to his voice just made the laughter I was stifling rise to the surface.

He saw the hopelessness of his position and started laughing with me. "I know you look much older that you are, but that was ridiculous," he managed as we tried to calm down.

"I think she knew I wasn't old enough and just wanted to prank you. She's probably laughing in the kitchen right now. She just wanted to get a look at your license so she could see your name. Did you notice the way she kept looking at you?"

"Yeah?" he asked, surprised. He then sat straighter in his chair, ran a hand through his hair and said, "I do look pretty good, don't I?"

"Yes, you do," I assured him. I knew he was trying to get a reaction out of me, but I didn't bite on that hook. It's too difficult to feign jealousy when you trust someone so completely.

The rest of diner was perfect. We talked about the animals hanging in the restaurant, the food, the service, but nothing important came up. We finished and went out to his truck. He didn't start the truck right away, but just sat there looking straight out the windshield. I knew he had something on his mind, and had all day. When he finally did turn to face me, I didn't have to wait any longer to find out.

He looked at me with a worried look in his eyes. He took my hand and kissed it sweetly before he began.

"I have something to give you, but I want to say something before I do." He stopped and laid his head on the back of the seat, looking skyward for strength.

"Is something the matter?" I asked quietly, holding my breath.

"No. I was just praying that I say this right," he said. The anticipation of what he was going to say sent a chill down my spine.

"Are you cold? I can turn the heater on," he caringly offered. I shook my head no and he continued. "At least put my jacket on. Your mother would kill me if I brought you home sick. She probably wouldn't let me see you again." He put his coat around my shoulders tenderly and I looked at him expectantly.

"That's actually what I want to talk to you about. You are quite younger than I am—"

"I thought that didn't matter to you." I interrupted. I was so sick and tired of hearing how old we were. I wanted to tell him to make up his mind: either it mattered or didn't.

"It doesn't. At least I didn't think about it until I got carded in there," he said, pointing to the restaurant. He shook his head, making up his mind, "It doesn't matter."

He reached into his pocket and pulled out his class ring from school. He held it up in the light so I could see it through the half-dark.

"I want to give this to you. Do you know what this means?" He asked. I nodded. I knew exactly what it meant, but I did not want to say anything he might interpret the wrong way. I knew he was in a difficult position and didn't want to make it more so.

"This means, to me anyway, that you're mine. I don't mean that in a physical sense. I mean…Oh hell. I don't even know what I mean, how can I expect you to?" He threw himself back against the door of the truck.

I could do nothing but watch. I knew what he was trying to say, but couldn't put it into words any easier. He held the ring in the palm of his hand and squeezed it over and over hoping that would give him his insight. He sat up suddenly and pointed to the clock on his stereo.

"That's what I'm talking about. This is what I want to give you. Time is the most precious thing on earth. I want it to count. I can't give you as much as I'd like to, so I'm giving you this instead. Not in place of my time, but to remind you that I love you when I have to give someone else my time."

He looked up at me and I saw tears in his eyes. He was so overcome by the power of his emotions; he cried. He picked up my hand and slid the ring onto my finger. He held it there for a moment. His head bent down again so I couldn't read his eyes. He was purposely hiding his eyes from me, not allowing me to see all that was unspoken within him. I hold that moment in time in my heart.

My thoughts, on the other hand, were screaming at me. Love and Hope being the two loudest. I loved him so much. 'Too much at times,' I told myself. So much so, it didn't feel like merely saying I love you would cover the depth of the emotion. And hope, I had too much hope as well. I hoped he would replace this ring with another. I hoped God hadn't put him in my life to give me a little taste of what was to come. I didn't want a taste. Nothing in all the great love stories I had read could compare to the way he made me feel.

This wasn't a storybook romance, though. This was my real life. My night in shining armor wasn't riding a white horse brandishing a sword to ward off any who might cause me harm. He was sitting in a pick-up truck, stroking my fingers lovingly with his thumb, crying at the strength of his love for me. Princes, I realized, could come in many shapes and sizes.

My thoughts had made me start to cry. I knew why he had struggled so to put his feelings into words. I now had the same problem. I stopped and reread my thoughts and found the answer was there all the time.

"I love you so much," I started. At the sound of my voice, he looked up from studying my hand. The emotion I saw there seeped into my soul. Not the emotion itself, but the intensity. His eyes glowed from the fire we had built in his heart. In our hearts. It was clear to me, at that moment, I had nothing to fear. I wasn't afraid of my love for him, from that second forward. I didn't have to fear taking a wrong turn and not finding my safety in the darkness of the unknown. He would be there, with me. He would light my way back to the path that lead straight into his arms. I felt stability wash over me, pick me up in its wave, and carry me forever towards him. I would never be scared of the light in his eyes. It was my beacon. It would show me the way. I could never be lost as long as the light glowed. Where ever he leads, I will follow.

"I love you so much," I started again, "That saying 'I love you' doesn't seem to cover how much I really do. You said time was the most precious thing on earth. If you add time to time, you end up with forever. And that is as long as I will love you."

He reached over and brushed my cheek with his fingers as if only by touching me could he be sure I was there with him. He enfolded me in his arms so quickly I lost my breath. His lips touched mine with an intensity to match his eyes and I was powerless to do anything but respond with an intensity of my own. We broke apart to catch our breath, then his lips moved again. This time they moved across my cheek and down my neck. I felt his warm breath in my ear. I arched my neck upward to meet his lips as they kissed their way from my collar to my lips once more.

It was my turn to let my lips wander. I followed the same route he had taken with me. I needed him to feel the same as I did. I needed him to feel the sensations he had just caused. I bit the lobe of his ear gently before I kissed my way down the side of his neck, under his chin, then up the other side of his neck to gently bite his other ear.

He breathed my name and the sound of it on his lips made me tremble. He put one hand on each of my shoulders and pushed me back to look into my eyes. "I love you," he fairly growled then pulled me back into his arms.

We cuddled together, whispering to each other. There wasn't another soul around, but neither of us wanted to break the quiet of the mood. He told me how he decided to buy that particular truck and a few other things that didn't pertain to anything in general. It felt so good to lean against him with his arm around me.

We both noticed the time: twenty-five minutes to eleven. Neither of us wanted the day to end, but we had to let reality in sooner or later. He started the truck and we headed for home.

The drive took about fifteen minutes, so we decided to talk for the last ten. It was such a shame to waste even a few minutes of precious time. We talked for too long because the outside light flashed off and on. We kissed goodbye and I started to get out of the truck when the lights flashed again. I walked to the door, closed it behind me, turned, and looked back out at him. The week ahead stretched out in front of me like the next fifty million years.

Once I got in the house, I realized that the state of euphoria I was in was to be short lived. My mother was livid.

"When I say be home by eleven o'clock, I mean in this house, not in the driveway. You know the rules. You can't go out with him next week." She was using the tone that meant nothing I said could change her mind.

I went to my room, not thinking this was the

right time to show her his ring, and got ready for bed. I could only think of the death sentence my mother just delivered me. If time was so important, and I didn't have it to give, how was I supposed to deal with the loss? I had to find a way to change my mother's mind. I had no idea how easy that would be.

Chapter Nine

The next day was Sunday. Just as in the Bible, it was a day of rest for us, also. I usually read in my room listening to my music while my parents read the paper and listened to their music in the living room. That day, my mother and I played a board game while waiting for my father to wake up from a nap. I casually reached for the die, but before I could roll, my mother took my hand and turned it over so she could see his ring.

"That's a pretty stone," she said nonchalantly. "When did you get that?"

"Last night," I returned, completing my turn.

She rolled the die and had her turn as she said, "It's getting more serious by the week, isn't it?"

I tried to decipher her tone, whether she approved or disapproved, but something in her eyes made me realize she liked him very much. I took my turn before I answered.

"Not by the week," I said. 'By the day,' I thought to myself. 'Why can't I tell her how I feel?'

"Has he tried anything?" she asked, more

concerned than nosey. She asked the question not like a question, but more of a confirmation in the trust she put in him. In us.

"No, Mom. It's not like that."

"Not like what?" she asked, pretending she had no idea what I was talking about.

"Sex isn't an issue with us," I tried to explain, not knowing what to expect out of her mouth next.

"And why is that?" she raised her eyebrows in question.

"It is so much more than that." I can't explain my relief that she nodded saying she understood what I meant. I had no other way of saying it.

She rolled the die. "Has he said he loves you, yet?" She moved her man across the board. "I'll buy it."

I gave her the property. "Yes." I rolled the dice.

"Have you told him? Twenty-five dollars rent."

"Yes, and it's doubled. You own all three."

"So, now what are you going to do? You

rolled doubles, go again."

"What do you mean? Luxury tax, nuts!"

"You know what your father's and my thoughts are about going steady. Please hand me the die."

"I know. You think it's the first step towards marriage. I own that."

"How much rent? It's true, you know. You're step-father and I went together for five years before we got married."

"I know. And he is *sixteen* years older than you are. But I guess with older people it doesn't matter," I tried to joke. "Here's your change."

"It mattered when we first saw each other, but not now. Go to jail, I hate that space."

"Well, it doesn't matter to us, now. Are you saying it should? Roll to see if you get doubles to get out."

"I'm not saying it should matter, just that you should think about it, both of you. I did it! Doubles!"

My mother had all the luck. My turn next.

"So, are you thinking about it? I own that one, my dear."

"About what? Twenty-five dollars doubled is fifty, here."

"Marriage. My turn."

"Are you trying to get rid of me?" I asked, trying to desperately turn the direction of this conversation to something else. Before I could give her the property she had bought, she put my hand down and covered it with hers.

"I'm not trying to do anything but make you think about the realistic side of things. If you love each other like you say, marriage is always a possibility."

'O.K.,' I reasoned with myself, 'we are having an honest conversation about a serious subject that I really need her advice about. Take a chance and open up a little.'

"Do you think he loves me?" I gingerly asked, half expecting an explosion. "I mean, really loves me?"

She looked me straight in the eyes and said, "I think he loves you very much."

"I do love him, Mom. But we are taking this one step at a time. Who knows? Maybe we will go together for five years before the subject even comes up." I reached for the die again. "He's my P.C., my Prince Charming. I wouldn't change anything about him. It is as if we are made for one another. Doubles, good, I can roll again."

"You do know this isn't one of your romance novels, don't you? That's mine, thirty bucks."

"Yes, and it may not have a happy ending. One, two, three…" I counted off the spaces as I moved my piece.

"Boardwalk," she said, nodding to the board, "that's a pretty big decision. Why don't you think about if for awhile."

I knew she wasn't talking about the property. And she was right, it was a big decision. I couldn't think about a happy ending, or any kind of ending. This was only the beginning. Hadn't he said that last night?

I looked from the board to the ring on my finger. Before I had gone to bed the previous night, I wrapped some yarn around the underside of it so it would fit on my finer. I could have worn it on the chain with my heart, but he had put it on my finger, and on my finger it was to stay.

I got up from the table and went to my room. My piece still sitting on the valuable property waiting for my decision. I didn't have one to give it. 'Buy boardwalk? You have got to be crazy to not buy boardwalk!' I began to myself. That's the big one. The space everyone prays to land on and buy. They count out what they need on the die to get there, shout victoriously when they finally land on it, gloat when collecting rents, build houses and hotels. There is no downside to Boardwalk.

Unless, rounding the board the eventual pitfalls catch up to you. Luxury tax, Go To Jail, rents along the way, and unexpectedly bad Chance cards. One bad turn around the board and you end up bankrupt, with everything gone, including Boardwalk. But is the chance of losing it a good enough reason for not buying to begin with? What happens if you pass on this turn, telling yourself you will buy it next time, and you never land on it again. Someone else will have taken advantage of the opportunity you let by. You take a chance, no matter which way you decide, and have to keep playing, Win or Lose.

'Stop comparing your life to a board game!' I shouted, pointing at myself in the mirror. Part of me wanted to march back out to the table and tell my mother I was buying the property, then bury her in hotels; but the part of me that won reached over and flicked on my radio. There was no use trying to concentrate on anything but him. The book I was reading was still on my dresser where I left it earlier. I had made a pledge not to over-analyze, and I let that promise go without as much as a backward glance. I permitted myself a tiny glimpse; a sliver of a hoped-for future to shine in. I closed my eyes and allowed myself to dream.

We never did finish that game.

The next week was boring. My classes went by slowly and the nights even slower. I had tried not doing any work and saving it for the weekend so the last night before I saw him would go by quicker at least, but all that did was put me that much farther behind. My class load was heavy enough. I couldn't afford to slip. After a meeting with my counselor, I had doubled-up all my classes and applied to go to college a year earlier. If I was accepted, this would be my last year of high school.

All I did was write my thoughts to him. The more I wrote him, the more I missed him. I tried working myself even harder by doing extra credit and student teaching during my free time, but I missed him then, also. I finally decided to keep to my routine. It would give me something to look forward and I could mark the days by what I did. 'Only three more showers until I see him next,' I would say to myself. Towards the end of the week, even that wasn't helping.

It had killed me to write him this letter, telling him I wouldn't be able to go to his friend's wedding with him because I was technically late on Saturday; but before I mailed it; my mother had the best news of the week for me.

I asked her for a stamp and she asked," Did you tell him you couldn't see him this weekend?"

"Yes, Mom. You don't have to remind me." That wasn't what I needed to hear. I was almost in tears at the thought.

"Your father and I talked it over and we decided that you were here on time last week and we know how you feel about each other, so you can go to the wedding."

I almost knocked her over, I hugged her so hard. "Besides, I couldn't stand you moping around here for another week." She was making light of something that was life or death to me. I didn't know if I should hug her again, or tell her to be serious.

"I guess I better not mail this letter, then," I said. I ran for my bedroom and immediately began a much happier letter.

I had some more wonderful news later that night. Something that would make the next days fly by even faster. My big sister from out of state called to say she and her children were coming up for a week and staying with us. I was so excited, I cleaned my room.

This particular sister and I were closer than any other in my family. When I was little, she used to stand across the room and holler my name while stretching her arms out for me. I would holler 'Buddy!' run and jump into her arms. It had been quite a few years since she could pick me up and throw me in the air, but we were still buddies. She arrived late Friday night, or early Saturday morning, and went right to bed.

She didn't get much sleep though, the children were up extra early jumping around with excitement. I got up when I heard their voices and decided the best plan was to get ready, then wait for him to arrive; rather than visiting and then rushing to get ready later.

Again, it was as if I had read his mind. I was bubbling to my sister that I would introduce him to her when he arrived and I saw her eyes glance over my shoulder. I instinctively looked behind me and saw him standing in the door, smiling at me. I ran to the door, opened it, and had to forcibly stop myself from throwing myself into his arms. I laughed and told him he was taking a big chance coming so early. He smiled again and said it was worth seeing the look on my face. I said a silent prayer of thanks to whomever it was that told me to get ready first.

My mother came into the kitchen and asked him why in the world he had showed up so early. I ran into my room to pack the few things I would need for the day. We had decided to get ready back at his house so as not to have to ride the whole way in uncomfortable clothes.

"I didn't want to get caught short on time to get my tux on before the wedding. Those things are hard enough without hurrying to put it on. Besides, I was up early and didn't want to sit around the house watching the clock," I heard him tell my mother. I finished throwing, and throwing is the key word there, things into my bag and grabbed a jacket. We said quick goodbyes to my family and were off. He started the truck and put it in gear, but didn't back up yet. He leaned over and gave me a big kiss.

"Is there a reason for this?" I asked between kisses, "Not that I'm complaining."

"I don't need a reason, remember?" He said, kissing me again. "I needed a recharge, anyways. I couldn't have made it back to my house without a kiss."

He laughed as I gave him one last kiss as we backed out of the driveway. Yep, my mother was in the window watching the whole thing, smiling.

"I wouldn't want us to get in an accident," I warned with yet another kiss.

"If you keep this up, I won't be able to concentrate on the road and we will get in an accident," he said. I pretended to be offended and moved as far over to my side of the seat as possible. He put up with this for less than two minutes. He reached over, grabbed my hand and hauled me across the seat to sit next to him, shifted the truck, then grabbed my hand again. He gave me a look that dared me to move over. I smiled innocently and gave his hand a squeeze. He smiled back mimicking me, then laughed.

I couldn't wait for him to tell me about the rehearsal diner. He had wanted to take me with him, but there was no way we could work that part of the weekend out. He burst out laughing and shook his head. "You know what I ended up doing? So many people asked me if you were coming, I ended up standing up and making an announcement 'Yes, she's coming.'" I shook my head with him. That is something I could absolutely picture him doing.

About an hour into the trip, something he said to me a few weeks earlier came back to haunt me, and had been haunting me most of the week.

Some of the things we had said to each other the last weekend were rattling around in my mind as well. And with the letter he had written me that week, I was developing an acute case of the nerves.

I had thrown his letter in my bag and reached down to fish around and find it, which was very difficult because he refused to let go of my hand. He looked very surprised when he realized what I was looking for, then I started to read a passage aloud.

'I had the definite taste of sole in my mouth (my foot). I hope I didn't. I remember tears. Mine were happy, I realized I had asked and received, but yours??? When I gave you my ring I said your mine (Yes, I am very possessive) But, big but, moreover it means I AM YOURS... Tell me how I can prove to you that, although I said your age mattered to me, your age doesn't. Sixteen or Twenty-one, it doesn't matter, You are a beautiful young woman in my eyes.'

I looked up when I finished reading to find him staring intently on the road in front of us. I wasn't sure how to ask what I wanted to know, but I had to have an answer.

"Are you sure you wouldn't rather have taken a knock-out to this wedding?" I shouldn't have asked so bluntly, but that is precisely what I wanted to know.

"Is that what is bothering you? I was wondering why you were so quiet," he said.

"I just don't want you to feel self-conscious about bringing me home, so to speak."

"Listen, I am only going to tell you this one last time. I have only taken one girl 'home to meet mother'. I have only told one girl 'I love you', and only one girl, no," he stopped just long enough to look at me to be sure I was listening as he finished, "Only one *woman* has ever worn my ring. That woman is you, got it?"

I nodded and put the letter back in my bag. I wasn't sure why, but his angry speech hadn't made me feel any better. Something inside me snapped. I moved over to my side of the truck and rounded on him like a caged tiger.

"Are you the only one who can have insecurities? I'm sorry. I forgot for a minute that I am so sure of myself I had no right to ask for confirmation of a few things. I'm so scared I'll probably throw up on the bride or something. Next time I will just assume things." I was so hurt and angry, and I couldn't define why. All I could do was turn away from him and look out the window.

I was beginning to feel a little silly about my outburst, but I had made a valid point. He was always writing how he was nervous about calling or seeing me for fear I wouldn't want to talk to him or tell him not to come. I had to reassure him that I definitely wanted to see him and was glad he had called. It felt to me that whenever I brought up my doubts, he would laugh them off and say I was being silly.

Did he think I had said 'I love you' to anyone else before him? He was the only man I had ever brought 'home to meet mother'. And his ring was the only ring I had accepted to wear. I felt slighted, and justly so.

Neither of us had said anything for a long, long time. I chanced a look at him to try to figure out what he was thinking. He saw me turn and said, "So, you're looking at me now?"

That remark made me more furious that the first one had. I wanted to cry with hurt and frustration. Mostly, I wanted him to turn around and take me home. I was not going to go through the whole day pretending to have a good time when we weren't even speaking.

"Well, say something," he said dryly. Just what was he expecting?

"What would you like me to say?" I asked coolly.

"Hell, I don't know. Just talk to me."

"It would have been a nice day for a wedding it if hadn't rained. I see a few breaks in the clouds, though. Maybe the sun will come out after all," I commented. At least I had followed orders. I had said something.

"That's not exactly what I had in mind," he said, shaking his head. I didn't know how infuriating that gesture could be until that moment.

"I'm not a mind reader," I replied. I was at the end of my rope, and I wanted him to know it.

"I know that, because if you knew what I wanted to do right now, you wouldn't be so smug," he ground out. Usually his temper intimidated me, but this time I lifted my chin and openly challenged it.

"And what would that be?" I asked, keeping my aloof appearance.

"I want to pull this truck over and paddle your ass!" he shouted back.

"And why would you want to do that?" I innocently asked. I knew he didn't make idle threats, but I was determined not to back down.

"Because you're acting like a spoiled brat!"

"I'm the spoiled brat?" I repeated, aghast. "Well, if being spoiled means I needed reassurance because I didn't want you to feel self-conscious about introducing me to your friends, then yes, I am spoiled."

"I thought I gave it to you," he growled back.

"I don't know what you thought you said, but that's not what I heard. I'm nervous enough without you hollering at me."

"I told you I loved you! What more do you want?"

"'I'm only going to tell you this one last time'. I didn't know I was on a limited supply. You made it sound like you were tired of saying it." That was it, I couldn't hold back the tears any longer. I tried desperately to hide them from him.

"I didn't mean it like that. I was just tired of you worrying about what everyone else thought of you when I should be the only one who matters. I wish to hell I never told you about that. I think you're beautiful, and if you don't measure up to their standards, who cares? You measure up, no, you *surpass* my expectations and..." he continued for a minute more before he heard me sniffling.

"Are you crying?" he asked, roughly. I looked further out the window in a vain attempt to hide my tears. "Look at me," he said. I knew by the sound in his voice I had better turn towards him.

"Why are you crying?" He asked.

'Why was I crying?' I asked myself, 'Didn't he hear the argument we just had?'

"Oh, come on, don't cry. I didn't mean it. Come here," he said, stretching out his free arm. He didn't have to ask me twice. I slid across the seat and buried my head in his shoulder.

"I'm sorry. I didn't mean to take your insecurities so lightly. I probably should have said what I did a little differently. I didn't mean to holler at you. Come on, stop crying."

He held me so close. I felt terrible about my outburst, but when he turned that impatient tone on me, when I was already feeling very vulnerable, I couldn't help losing my temper. Now I didn't know how to apologize for flying off the handle like that. I slid my arms around him and hugged him close.

"Feeling better?" he said supportively when I eventually lifted my head from his shoulder. I nodded and we rode in silence again. Only this time it was a serene quiet.

"I just had a thought occur to me, " he said suddenly. "We just had our first fight."

"That's nothing to be proud of," I joked.

"Do you know what that means?" he asked.

"That we both have very short tempers?" I tried lamely. I didn't know what he was getting at.

"It's official now. We are definitely in love, a real couple."

He was smiling! I couldn't grasp what he was talking about until I remembered something my father said to me once: 'You don't really know a person until you've argued with them'. I never knew what he meant until then.

"Does this mean we can make up?" I asked.

I snuggled a little closer and nuzzled his neck.

"I guess so," he agreed, chancing taking his eyes off the road to kiss me. "I found out one good thing about you," he said, mysteriously.

"Something good came out of all this?" I ran the argument back through my mind, but couldn't find a single good thing in it.

"Now I know you fight dirty," he laughed. "I would have won this one, too, if you hadn't started crying."

"What do you mean 'this one'? Are there going to be others?" We had hardly gotten past this one and he was already laying battle plans for the next one.

"There are bound to be others, realistically. But the making up is nice," he said, pulling me close to him again.

"We don't have to fight to do this, you know," I said. I stretched up to kiss his ear, then kissed my way down his neck to his collar.

"I know, boy, do I know! But if you want to make it to this wedding in one piece, you'll stop so I can concentrate," he groaned. I gave him one last kiss, then slid back to my side of the truck. He rolled down his window, muttering something about needing air.

I looked at him surprised, then decided I should concentrate also. Not on the road, but on what to say to his family. I pulled out my compact and tried to fix my make up the best I could without starting all over again. I took a side-long glance at him, still surprised. The possibility that I could have such a strong effect on him had never occurred to me. After all, weren't we learning all this together? Could it be feasible that my touch affected him the way his did me?

I would have continued with this line of thinking if an almost catastrophe hadn't happened. It had sprinkled a little, 'left over from the storm we passed' I thought. He flicked a switch on the dashboard to turn his windshield wipers on to see the road clearly, instead of peering through the droplets that hung to the glass. They swished up, then stopped. I looked at him quickly, not knowing what to say or do.

He reached forward and flicked the switch, trying to get them to spark into action, but nothing happened. "Oh, come on," he said, trying the switch again.

"This may sound like a stupid question," I said gingerly, "But, are they broken?"

"Look's like it," he said, vainly trying the switch again.

"Does everything else work?" I asked, wondering what else could go wrong.

"Looks like it," he said again, running a cursory check.

I began to get a little nervous. I started to imagine walking to his house, wet and cold, only to find he had missed the wedding. And when he was part of the wedding party, I didn't want that to happen. I asked worriedly, "Can we make it to your house?"

"Yeah, we'll make it there. I hope my dad will let me borrow his truck to get to the church, then to get you home."

'Getting home,' I thought. All I could hear was the tone in my mother's voice when she told me I was grounded for life. My imagination then went into overdrive. I could just picture myself hitchhiking or taking a bus home. The thought was so ridiculous I started laughing.

"I'm glad you can laugh at a time like this," he said wryly.

"I was just picturing myself walking home." I started giggling again. "I could probably flash a little leg and get some truck driver to drop me off right at my front door."

"You aren't flashing anything!" he growled. "I'll get you home, safe and sound. I'll just need a minute to figure out how," he finished softer than he started.

"I'm sure you will," I said. I tried to sound confident and trusting in him.

Apparently, it worked. He smiled and gave me my look, then said, "I just hope it doesn't rain again."

Chapter Nine

We drove the 'wrong' way around the block
when he reached his house. One of his friends, the
already married one, was going to stop by before
the wedding. "He usually drives up to the house
from the other way, so hopefully he won't notice
the wipers and razz me about it." I took one last
look at the truck before we entered the house. I felt
a bit sorry for it. I had always thought it was a very
sharp looking vehicle. But sitting there, with its
wipers hanging limply off the windshield, it looked
lost and abandoned.

Seconds later, the truck's feelings were the
farthest from my mind. We had walked from the
safety of each other's private company through the
door into a flurry of activity. He had warned me
that they had a house full of people, but I couldn't
have realized how full until we walked right into the
middle of it.

He asked someone where his mother was.
He heard her voice in the kitchen and headed for her
like a thirsty man heads for water. I stood alone for
a minute, feeling very much deserted. 'Pull
yourself together,' I firmly told myself. 'You can

handle this!' I never got the chance to. I heard someone call my name; or what I thought was my name. I had forgotten that his little sister's name was the same as mine. We both answered "Yes?" at the same time. All the people in the living room looked at each other in surprise, and laughed uproariously. I tried to not be embarrassed, it was funny. It broke the ice, though, and for that I was grateful. I looked into the kitchen from where I was standing and saw him talking to his mother. I could tell by the way he was holding his shoulders that he was telling her about his truck. I thought I saw her hide a smile.

He turned around and they both walked into the living room. His mother waved in greeting before she asked about the ride down. I smiled a secretive smile and answered, "It was interesting."

He checked the time then asked his sister if I could use her room to change. It was occupied by friends of the family, so his mother showed me hers. I took a quick look around to make sure there was a mirror, and thanked her.

I never changed so fast in my life. I couldn't see any point in making him wait for me, but I found when I emerged from the room that he hadn't even started changing yet. His mother looked at me with a very surprised expression on her face.

"Very nice," she said. "That is a very pretty dress."

I thanked her graciously. I didn't see any point in telling her I had raided three sister's closets to find this particular dress. It was a light aqua green with a high, Victorian neckline. The hem came to just below the knee, and with the puffed sleeves and gathered close at the wrist, it was a very form-flattering dress. I had chosen a simple pair of black pumps to show off my legs, and I must say, it had the desired effect. If they wanted a knock-out, then a knock-out they would get.

I took a seat at one end of the couch. Not knowing what a safe topic would be, I listened for my cue in the conversation around me.

"How are the twins doing?" his father asked me. I could not have been more shocked. I replied that they were fine and followed up with a question of my own.

"He told you about that?"

I didn't think that would be a funny question, but by the way they were all laughing, it must have been.

"Oh, yes," his mother answered. "He said he didn't want to go but that you grabbed his hand and dragged him out there. You look surprised."

"I didn't think he talked about me at home," I answered simply.

"Talk about you? We can't get him to shut up!" one brother boasted.

"He also said he had a surprise for you, but wouldn't tell us," his mother said. I thought for a minute before I answered. I wasn't sure if he wanted them to know he had given me his ring, but *I* wanted them to know.

"Well, maybe this?" I asked, holding up my hand so they could see his ring there. For one brief minute, I found myself wishing there was a different type of ring there. I felt a little self-conscious about it, but the look on her face wasn't surprise. It was as if she knew all along and just needed confirmation. Her look was saying, "I thought so."

He came down stairs, took one look at me,

turned around and ran back upstairs. He came down a few minutes later carrying his tie. Then there was a knock at the door. His friend had finally arrived.

"What happened to your tuck?" he asked him. He hadn't even fully made it through the door when he jumped on him.

"You noticed that, did you?" I asked.

"You can't help but notice it," he laughed. "The wipers are hanging off the windshield!"

"I parked it like that on purpose so you wouldn't see it, but you had to pick today to come the other way, didn't you?" I could see he was getting embarrassed. This was another side to him that I had never seen. He seemed so at ease in his home, but so tense about his friend busting on him. He seemed to take it well enough, though, like he had had to put up with it a lot growing up.

He introduced us and his friend said hello. I was a bit shocked at his reaction. His friend asked me how the ride down had been, other than the wipers, and I answered him rather easily. He looked at me with an expression of disbelief, as if he was saying to himself, 'This isn't the same girl who cried on the way down here because she was so nervous." I'm glad he didn't want to hold hands at that point. I don't think I could have unclenched my fingers from each other where I was holding them in my lap.

When he was finally ready, his mother announced she wanted a picture of the two of us. We stood up against the wall like prisoners at an execution. He had this withdrawn aura about him and I was starting to feel unsure of myself again.

His mother put her camera down and looked at us impatiently. "Move closer," she said. She looked through the viewer, "Hold hands," she directed. We both looked down and watch our hands clasp, then we looked back up and smiled. I never knew having a picture taken could be so exhausting.

His father had lent him his truck to get to the church, so I grabbed my coat and followed him out the door. He was walking so fast, I had to ask him to either slow down or pick me up and carry me. He looked back and said something about not wanting to be late.

"I don't want to be the last one there. I hate

that!"

I remember bits and pieces of the actual ceremony. I smiled at him when he looked at me from the front of the church where he stood with the rest of the bridal party. He smiled back, but it never reached his eyes. He looked back at his two friends bonding themselves together for life. I took for granted that he was incredibly nervous, standing there in front of a church full of people, but there was something else.

The ushers were escorting the guests out of the church when he waved to me to come stand next to him. I must have looked back blankly because he looked up to heaven for strength. He motioned that I should walk around to the empty row in front of me and stand next to him.

"You don't have to stand way over there," he said. He took my hand and we waited for the rest of the guests to file out. He must have needed one of the recharges only I could give him.

When we reached the reception, I was looking desperately for the rest of his family. I didn't know a soul there other than them. I was picturing myself wandering aimlessly around looking for them, when his mother found me and showed me where they were sitting.

I had told him earlier that when the wedding party was introduced, I was going to scream and cheer and generally embarrass him. But when he walked by to sit at the head table, I politely clapped and winked at him as we walked by. I knew I would have embarrassed myself more than him if I made a scene, but I wanted him to sweat a little.

The reception was very nice. The bride had made all the flowers herself and decorated the hall. Everything looked beautiful. After everyone had finished eating, he came over to sit beside me. He had gotten himself a beer and took off his tux coat. Now that the 'official' duties were finished, he looked like his old self again, much more relaxed. He leaned back in his chair and reached for my hand while he told me about certain people. Who was whose dad or girlfriend or boyfriend. Nothing was as funny as when I found out that almost everyone there knew about the wipers on his truck.

The commotion on the dance floor told all the single ladies that it was time to throw the bouquet. His little sister grabbed my hand and pulled me towards the floor. I declined at first, not wanting to get tangled in that mess, but she wasn't taking no for an answer. I looked at him, completely lost. I told him if I went up there, I was really going to try to catch it, praying he would tell me not to go. He pointed to the gathering of girls and said, "If you don't hurry, you'll miss it."

I followed his sister, but when I tried to hide in the back, she pushed me up front. The maid-of-honor was standing beside me. The bride threw and it came straight for us. As it went sailing by, the ribbons caught around my fingers. When I looked down, the bouquet was lying at my feet. I picked it up and handed it to the maid-of-honor. The band leader saw me trying to get rid of it and immediately started in on me. I was told to stand aside so the single men could try for the garter.

He walked past me and almost didn't look at me. I was terrified. I had never seen him look so intent. Intent on catching the garter, or intent on trying to keep what little dignity he had left intact, I'm not sure which.

The band did a count down and the groom threw. The man I love… just stepped out of the way and let it land on the floor. I couldn't exactly see from my chair off to the side, but it looked like, to me, when he moved out of the way, he tripped and fell.

'Good!' I thought, 'I hope he broke something!' I was in such a state of shock I never noticed who actually did catch the garter. It turned out to be a young kid. I was being called back out onto the floor so he could put the garter on my leg. The band played a strip tease beat as he slid it up. When he reached my knee, I stood up and almost knocked him over. I ripped the thing off and handed it back to the kid and walked away.

After he had dusted himself off from his fall, he had walked off the floor without a backward glance and didn't stick around to see the kid and me. As he walked by the band, the leader said, "That poor guy wanted it so bad, he dove for it!"

I wanted everyone to know that he loved me so much, he just stepped out of the way, so I said, "That's my boyfriend."

The minute those words were out of my mouth I regretted them. The band had a field day with that one. After I returned to my seat, I purposely didn't sit next to him, but a chair on the other side of the table. The band noticed it and said, "Uh,oh. It looks like that relationship is in trouble." They didn't know the half of it.

He reached across the table and took my hand. "Aren't you going to say anything?" he timidly asked.

"Why? Do you know how embarrassing that was?" I was embarrassed to a point I'd never been before. I was confused and hurt as to why he just let the garter go by. And this whole situation happened because I wasn't honest in the beginning and stick to my original decision to not get involved in the first place with the garter/bouquet mess.

He said, "Come on," and stood up. I laid the bouquet on the table and followed him. I didn't have much of a choice; he had one of his grips on my hand. The band made yet another wisecrack as we walked for the door. Neither of us paid any attention.

I started to get very scared. I had no idea what was going through his mind. Was he taking me outside to yell at me for embarrassing him? Was I making an already difficult day even harder

for him? My heart was racing with dread. For all I
knew, he was taking me home right then.

We walked out the door and a few feet into
the parking lot before he stopped. He turned me
around and tilted my head to his.

"I'm sorry," he said. He looked so scared
and vulnerable that my intentions to stay mad at
him simply vanished. I dug around deep in my
mind trying to find a single one to hold on to, but
there were none to be found. I felt exhausted and
defeated. Once more, his eyes had told me
everything I wanted to know. I had one more
question, though, and the answer could only come
from him.

"If you didn't want me to catch the bouquet,
you should have told me. That's why I asked. If
you didn't want to catch the garter, you should have
told me that, too. Instead you stepped out of the
way." I looked down, disappointed. Not that he
hadn't caught it, but that he hadn't told me. I
thought we could tell one another anything. Isn't
that what we said, anything in the world and we
would understand?

"Is that what you think? That I stepped out

of the way?" he asked, looking at me with those eyes. Eyes full of love and disbelief. I nodded. "I didn't. The guys behind me wanted me to catch it and pushed me. I tripped and landed on the floor. When I got up, I saw who had caught it. I don't want to sound like I'm making excused for myself, but I couldn't help it."

He dropped his hands from my shoulders. It would have been a pretty lame excuse if something in his voice hadn't told me to believe him. His apology was as sincere as I have ever heard. I had one final question before I closed the case forever.

"Did you want to catch it?" I asked quietly.

"I don't know," he said. I couldn't find any fault with his answer. He was being honest. I wanted an answer and I got it.

He stood in front of me for a moment more before he took my hand. With both of our hands together, he again tipped my head up until my eyes met his. He was searching for his answers in my eyes like I had in his. I knew he was waiting for me to say something, anything. I didn't trust my voice to let any words out without shaking. I looked at him, lost in his eyes for an eternity, until I knew what he wanted to hear.

"I love you," I whispered. I watched his eyes change instantly from sorrowful to passionate. He bent his head down and pressed his lips to mine gently. He felt he couldn't trust himself to kiss me with all the feelings he felt right then. I stood up on my toes to continue the kiss when he would have stopped. I heard him let out one haggard breath before he wrapped his arms around me and took command of the kiss. Standing on my toes made me lose my balance and I slipped my arms around his neck. He held me even closer, catching me before I could fall. He molded our bodies together so not even a whisper could have passed between us. He ran his tongue over my cheek to my ear and would have gone further when we heard voices.

"We can't do this here," he said, taking a very deep breath. I nodded saying I understood. He held me close to him for a split second more. He seemed torn between going back inside to the party or taking me off where we could be alone. I knew that look, that posture, that aura. He definitely had something on his mind. But like he had just said, not here.

He gave me one last kiss, this one much more respectable, then opened the door for us to reenter the restaurant.

The rest of the day passed without incident. I can honestly say, after we both relaxed, we had a genuinely good time. I made some really, really bad jokes. We attempted to dance together, to which the band made the comment, "Aww, all better now." He told me he'd teach me to ski. Before we knew it, it was late afternoon and things were winding down. Before we left, he introduced me to the bride and groom. In the excitement of the morning, neither of us thought it would be a good idea. I wished them both a happy forever as he explained that we were leaving. I knew he was his old self again when he started exaggerating about the long, long, long drive he had ahead of him. I felt like smacking him for that, but when I turned to give him a piece of my mind, he asked me what time it was. I automatically looked down to my wrist where my watch always was before I remembered I had taken if off that morning. Yep, he thought that was very funny.

In the truck on the drive down he had

noticed me looking at my watch. It was very large and had a mini-calculator built into it. What can I say, I was a bookworm. He looked at it with semi-disgust and said, "Are you going to wear that today? It makes you look like a free-eekin' brain." I told him I had no intention of wearing it, it didn't match my dress. At that time I didn't think another thing about it, but I was to find out what a big deal he would make out of it. All day he would ask me what time it was, then laugh when I looked at my empty wrist. It was all right in my mind, though. It would have stopped being so funny, but I fell for it *every* time.

He started his father's truck and drove in the direction we had come that morning. He turned his blinker on with a flick of his wrist and took us up a side road. When I asked him where we were headed, his only reply was that he wanted me to see something.

As he began slowing down, he pointed out the window to the right of us. It was a beautiful A-frame house, with a for sale sign out front. I couldn't believe my eyes. Why was he showing me a house? I knew why.

"Do you like it?" he asked when I turned to look at him.

He drove up further so I could get a better view. "Well?" he waited expectantly.

My first reaction was to throw myself into his arms and ask, "Is this going to be our home?"

I settled for asking shakily, "Is this the house your thinking of buying?"

"I'm thinking about it," he said quietly, mysteriously, looking out the windshield intently.

"I like it. It doesn't have much of a front yard, but it looks like a friendly house."

He chuckled at the fact that only I would describe a house as friendly, but he understood what I meant. He drove further up the road, the pulled into a clearing of tree hidden from the road. If he hadn't already known it was there, he would have driven right past it.

"I want to talk about this," he said, holding up the bouquet from the seat between us. I had thought we had resolved the situation, but he wanted to reopen the case.

"What would you like to know?" I asked, wary of the way his eyes were changing so rapidly.

"Do you know what they say about the people who catch them?" he questioned. I had to look away from him. His eyes were revealing far too much.

"You can't even look at me?" he asked desperately. I looked up at him and immediately wished I hadn't.

"It means they are the next to get married," he answered his original question. "Are you ready for that?"

I had no quick answer for him. My mother was right. That still ticks me off.

Was I ready for marriage? The question hung in the air. I had dreamed of a future with him and hoped for this moment. But now that it was here, I had no words. My mind wandered back to the night before the fair when I had said the first thing that came to my mind, then had to convince him it was true. If I told him I was ready, would he take me seriously? Or break my heart by not believing me? I had dreamed of a wedding like the one we had just attended, but I was looking past the day, and into the lifetime behind it. This question required a much longer and serious conversation than I wanted to start right then.

Was he, in his round-about way, asking me to marry him? Wait, maybe I was reading too much into this. He could be asking if I was ready for people to know we were that serious about each other. 'Did he ever actually ask the question?' I asked myself. The answer is no.

That had to be it, I was reading too much into this. If he ever said the words, I mean, actually asked me the question, I knew my answer would be yes. But until then, my only answer was, "I don't know."

"Neither do I," he said, leaning back in the seat. We sat in silence, each occupied with their own thoughts. He started the truck and said, "We better get going. We wouldn't want everyone to beat us back to the house when we left before they did. There would be too many questions."

We pulled off the side road and started for his home. He looked at me and offered his hand. I slipped my hand into his and drove the rest of the way quietly.

There isn't much else to tell about that day. We changed at his house and visited with his family after they returned from the wedding reception. We noticed the time and decided to leave. The drive home was uneventful, except for the weather.

We arrived at my house a full thirty minutes late because of the dense fog that had descended when we got further north on the highway. Furious isn't a strong enough word to describe how my mother felt.

I was so exhausted from the trip and emotions I had to sort through. If he is sitting next to me, I know the answer. But when he is miles away, I don't think I could have answered what two and two were. A good night's sleep was just what I needed. I would deal with everything in the morning.

Chapter Ten

The next morning, I barely had a chance to finish breakfast before my mother said she wanted to discuss the night before. Discussing something with my mother meant you sit while she talks and nod your head occasionally to let her know you are still listening. This time was a little different, she had enlisted an accomplice. My sister, my buddy, my idealistic portrait of the working mother and wife, had taken the seat beside my mother on the opposite side of the table from me. For the first few minutes, I sat patiently waiting for my cue to speak. I knew both women and my boyfriend were right. It didn't matter how late or how much time it would have wasted finding a phone, I should have called.

"You're right," I agreed, when my turn came. That took them both by surprise. Looking at this through my mother's eyes, the panicker, I could have been laying in a ditch somewhere, or being held against my will, or any other terrible things she could have dreamed up in those thirty minutes. I felt bad I had made her worry and apologized for not thinking of her peace of mind. There was no way of defending my actions, because they were wrong. I threw myself on the mercy of the court.

The court did have mercy, this time. Instead of grounding me from everything except breathing, she just said I couldn't go out the upcoming weekend. She might as well have grounded me from breathing, he was like air to me.

After that, I gave up. There was no arguing with her when she used that tone. I also knew that if I did, she would add more time. I decided to take what I had, and go for the appeal another time. A wise decision I still agree with today.

We had made plans to go to a village in Canada where they lived life in the pioneer's days. My mother had taken the last few minutes we had before leaving to have our 'discussion' and we were waiting for my father to give us the 'go' sign. My father walked into the kitchen just then and shocked all three of us in the room by asking my sister, "So, what did you think of the man who is going to marry your sister?"

My father walked into the kitchen just then and shocked all three of us in the room by asking my sister, "So, what did you think of the man who is going to marry your sister?"

"Dad!" was all I could manage.

I looked from him to Mom in surprise. My dad was standing in the kitchen smiling, waiting for an answer from my sister.

My dad took the whole scene in and smiled even more. I don't know what he found so funny, but he started laughing. "Seems to me, if a young man is considering marriage, buying a house would be the way to start."

I looked from my dad to my mother. She tried to look disappointed, but she couldn't. She half-smiled and said, "Your dad is never wrong."

"Don't you want to marry him?" he asked.

Oh, this was *not* the way I wanted to have this conversation with them. We were leaving momentarily for a trip to another country, and he wanted to start this now?

"I'm not marrying him," I said, hoping that would be the end of it.

"Then why are you dating him?" he asked. "The only reason to date a fellow is to see if he is marriage material. Why make him drive all the way up here if you aren't serious?" he asked. I told you they were old fashioned in their thinking.

'Damn, that backfired, didn't it?' I thought. Wasn't I just in this position yesterday when he asked me the same thing after showing me the house?

"I want to see him. We have fun and …" I started slowly. I didn't know where to go from there.

Dad jumped in with a question. "Don't you think he wants to marry you?" he said, smiling.

"I know he does." My answer was so confident, I could see my mother slouch out of the corner of my eye.

"How do you know that? Has he talked about it?" She asked.

"He showed me the house he wants to buy," I answered. Now that this was started, I was going to see it through. I couldn't be honest with her about my feelings before. About a subject this serious, I was determined now to have everything out in the open.

"When? Yesterday?" she asked, slouching even further.

"You are too young to be even considering the possibility of getting married," I heard my sister say from the other side of the room.

That irritated me. I can't think of any other word to describe it. 'You live three states away, come into town after not having seen me for two years, meet him for five minutes, overhear a conversation, and then decide you have to have an opinion?' I yelled at her, in my mind of course. I looked at her out of the corner of my eye and said, "You aren't in this!" and to the rest of the interested parties I said. "How about when he and I decide what we're doing, we'll let you know."

My dad took the whole scene in and smiled even more. I don't know what he found so funny, but he started laughing. "Seems to me, if a young man is considering marriage, buying a house would be the way to start."

"I knew I shouldn't have let you go yesterday," my mother groaned.

"She could do worse," dad laughed. "Now, you aren't giving her enough credit." He turned to my mom, "Isn't she applying to go to college next year rather than the year after? Doesn't she take care of kids everyday after school? She takes care of kids in school by teaching there, doesn't she?"

When my mother nodded, he continued, "Seems to me the only objection you have is age. She may be only 16 in years, but in terms of responsibility she is 21 or more. She's got a good head on her shoulders. You raised her right. She's brought home a decent, well-brought-up young man who makes a good living and goes to mass." He turned to me, "Would you agree with that?"

Shocked, all I could do was nod. I had no idea my quiet step-father had put this much thought into this, much less be helping me with my mother.

"So, what are you going to say if he asks you?" Dad said to me, winking.

"If he asks me, I will say 'yes'." Another confident answer, this one almost put my mother in tears.

"He'll ask you," my dad said, nodding at me confidently.

My dad took the whole scene in and smiled even more. I don't know what he found so funny, but he started laughing. "Seems to me, if a young man is considering marriage, buying a house would be the way to start."

"Now that that's settled, you ready to go?"

my dad said, heading for the door.

That village in Canada is also on my list of places to go back to.

I can't say too much about school that week. Same teacher upset by my not taking notes, same annoying guy in the locker next to mine. Same old same old. I was getting nervous about Friday. He wouldn't get my letter until he got home, and he stopped before that. He also called on Thursday night to see if the plans for the weekend had changed, but I never got a call that week. I was sure he would stop, and Mom would cause a scene. But after the conversation with my dad, she had promised to try to look at things differently. As far as I knew, I was a grounded adult with a curfew. To say the least, my nerves were fried.

I had the worst possible day of school. I locked my combination lock backwards on my locker and had to have a janitor cut it off. I was late for class, and the teacher made me make up the time, which made me late for the next class, and on and on. We had a substitute bus driver that night and, because I was the last person off the bus, I told him where all the stops were. I think I scarred a kindergarten student for life when I almost forgot his stop. Finally, I reached home. I found a letter from him there. I turned the letter over and noticed the date. He had written me every day that week. 'This would have been a big weekend,' I thought, miserable.

I had to chuckle to myself. As bad of a day as I thought I was having, he had had worse. He wrote earlier that week about the time he had after the wedding. Of course, it being Sunday, he couldn't do anything about getting his truck fixed. He decided to give it a try getting all the way up to work. He rigged a string through the wipers, then through the window so he could make them work if it rained. As clever as I thought that was, his arms must have been killing him when he finally arrived at work. He had tried to stop at the bank machine to get out money for the week, which of course was broken. So when Monday night rolled around, he decided rather than getting a motel room for the night, he would try to make it home and take care of things from there. When he got there, exhausted and broke, his mom had told him she wanted to talk.

Knowing this talk was coming for a while now, he said in his letter, he stayed up and had a heart-to-heart with her. He said in his letter he would tell me all about it when he saw me because it was too much to try and write all out.

I knew exactly what he meant. To explain all that happened at my house would take an entire notebook. What triggered both sets of parents to bring up the same subject on the same weekend? 'Seeing us together,' I said to myself. 'Seeing the way we look at each other, hold each other, care for each other. You would have to be blind not to see it.'

I flopped into the kitchen chair I was standing next to when I realized I was still staring at his letter. I didn't feel like taking it into my room and reading it there like I normally do. I leaned back in the chair I was sitting in, opened it, and the first words on the page read: 'Do you know how much I miss you? Do you know how in love I am with you? Do you know how much I need to hold you in my arms; hear your voice in my ears; feel your lips against mine? Before you, I didn't need anyone—But-- Do you know how much I need you?'

I held the letter up to my face, somehow trying to feel closer to them. I needed to hug him, but as all I had were his words, I held them instead. I was swept up by the surge of energy that coursed through me. I jumped up and took my things into my room. After dumping them on the floor, I reread his letter. Leisurely this time, savoring every word. I came to one part and I had to stop my jaw from dropping open. "The sun just came out and it feels sooo good (Notice only four o's) Your hugs (When I hold you) you need about fifty million o's in your 'so'. I gotta stop talking (writing) like this. It makes me feel (need) as if you're right here. When my memory is working, it is very vivid. Right now I'm remembering when we were in the car taking you home Sat. night. You asked me why I hadn't wanted you to pull (tug) the hairs on my arm (chest) at home. I told you, not in so many words, but, that your touch just starts to turn-me-on. You then seemed a little surprised and proceeded to say something like "I don't need to show you what else I can do, do I?" and then kissed my ear. I gotta stop this!!! You're two hours away and you're turning-me-on. I'm going to lunch. It'll give me a chance to cool down!!!!!!!!!'

While we were visiting with his family after the wedding, I wanted to be a little minx and annoy him like he had all day by asking me what time it was. All I could think of doing was discreetly pulling on the hairs on his arm. He looked at me and took his arm away, then held both of my hands so I couldn't do it again.

Later, in the car, he was teasing me about the way I sneezed. I didn't have a very lady-like sneeze and I usually sneezed five or six times in a row. I figured that if it had worked once, it would work again. I reached over and pulled very hard. He grabbed my hand and tucked it under his leg so I couldn't move while he tickled me mercilessly, the best he could and drive at the same time. He had very powerful legs and, trying my best, I couldn't move my hand. I agreed to be 'good' and he let me have my hand back. I cuddled up to him and asked him why he didn't like it.

"It's not that I don't like it," he said. "I like it, too much. That's why I didn't want you doing it at the house."

It took me a minute to figure out what he was saying, but when I did, I felt so stupid I hadn't figured it out before. He found me desirable. The thought itself was amazing. Here was a handsome, well-built, intelligent man, despite his denying it, who could have any woman he wanted, and he wanted me.

The same argument would be valid for his loving me. I knew he loved me, but thinking I was a turn-on for him was new. 'He had said that sex wasn't an issue,' I told myself. When he said that, I had pushed those thoughts far away in my mind. It was time, I decided, to bring them up front a little further. What I had told him when we first met was true, also. I wasn't a virgin. I had heard so much about it and my friends were talking about it all the time. When the opportunity arose, I decided to just get it over with. But this was a mature man who loved me, not a goofy, awkward teenager; that made all the difference in the world. I was having extreme difficulty getting past the fact that he found me desirable.

I had decided to add an air of mystery to the situation to heighten his curiosity. I didn't want to jump into bed with him when I first met him, and I didn't then. But I wanted to give him something to think about. "I don't need to show you what else I can do, do I?" I breathed into his ear, running my hand up his arm.

I had no idea what I would have done if he had pulled the car over and said, "Yes, show me." I truthfully didn't know a thing about that particular subject. A person can do it, and not even know what they'd done, as was my case. I knew what I had done, don't get me wrong, I didn't see what the big deal was, though. I knew that, with him, it would be a big deal. I would be the most moving and emotional act. I wanted us to learn that together, too.

He had said, "No, not if you want to make it home tonight."

I looked up from the letter and studied my appearance in the mirror above my dresser. I had short hair at the time, brown in color. I wore it brushed back on the sides and layered in the back. My eyes could never decide on a color. When I was happy or feeling excited about something, they would be blue. If I was angry or had something on my mind, they flashed bright green. He used to love to watch my eyes after we had kissed. They were so green he could see sparks in them, he would say, like emeralds shining in the sun.

I had an ordinary looking nose and mouth. My lips weren't full or seductive or any other provocative adjectives. I had what I counted as a '7' body. I didn't have an over-sized bust or curvaceous hips, but I did have long, slim legs. With seven older sisters, I had learned how to accentuate my flattering qualities, and play down my bad points. I wore my make-up to show off my eyes and clothes that flattered my figure.

I gave myself another good once-over and shook my head. I still couldn't get past the thought that he wanted to make love to me. The notion that I turned him on took my breath away.

Right then, I realized exactly how he felt. He was two hours away and I couldn't get my mind off him. I tried to pick out some clothes to wear the next day to get him off my mind. It didn't work.

Friday afternoon came quicker than I had

233

expected. I was so nervous I was shaking. I
realized I was always shaking over him, in one form
or another. My mother told me that if he showed
up, I would have five minutes to explain the
situation to him, and then he would have to leave. I
tried to condense what had transpired the past week
into five minutes, but couldn't. I was so frustrated I
just stood in front of the picture windows in our
living room and prayed he wouldn't come. That
sounds strange to say: hoping he *wouldn't* stop to
see me. If he never showed up, I would be spared
the embarrassment of having to send him home. If
he did show up, we could at least see each other and
make the best of what little, very little, time we had.

The time came and went that he usually
showed up. It was raining and the storm made night
driving with bad wipers even worse. I was getting
very worried.

At eight o'clock, I had enough waiting. I
got my wallet where I still kept his number. If he
was home, I wanted to give him a piece of my mind
for not calling. If he wasn't there, maybe they had
at least heard from him.

His mother answered the phone. I asked if

he was there. When she said he wasn't, my imagination went into overdrive. I told her that he wasn't with me either. I could see him lying in a ditch, bleeding to death somewhere. I must have been talking very fast because she started laughing.

"He called earlier," she said after I had finished. "They are working late tonight and they want to work half a day tomorrow. He said he would have called you, but he didn't have your number with him. He also said he would stop and see you after work tomorrow."

I thanked her and hung up. I hoped I hadn't been rude hanging up so quickly, but I was so relieved he was all right. 'He picked a great week to forget my phone number,' I told myself, cursing his bad memory.

My parents had decided to go out for a little while that night; and when they returned, the first question my mother asked was if he had stopped. I explained to her that he was working late and half the day tomorrow. She understood the fact that I had accepted not seeing him this week. All week, if I did something around the house, she would say, "That won't help you."

I tried to tell her I was so bored that even house work looked good to me, I'm not sure she bought it. I went to bed around nine o'clock, not wanting to stay awake with nothing to do. Again, I thanked whoever gave me that idea. I needed the extra sleep for the events of the next day.

Chapter Eleven

When I woke up the next morning, I realized I would have to go through the worrying all over again. I still had to tell him I couldn't see him in five minutes or less. I had to pray he would or wouldn't come and weigh the pro's and con's just as I had the night before. In a way, I wished he had come the night before. Then this would all be behind me.

Shortly before he was to arrive, I smiled at the sense of déjà vu I had as I took up my post at the picture windows. After waiting an hour, instead of my imagination going wild, my common sense kicked. They probably decided to work a full day.

As my mother and I were waiting for my father to get ready for mass, she told me her news. She explained that it was enough for her to know I had accepted the consequences of my actions; she couldn't hurt me by making me go through with it. She and my father had talked it over and, knowing how we felt about each other, I could see him if he showed up.

"He will, Mom. He will," I promised. I had every faith in the world that he would.

We hadn't been home from church more than fifteen minutes when he pulled into the driveway. I walked out the door to greet him with a murderess look on my face. He saw me coming and ducked quickly back into his truck, hiding.

I made a grab for the door handle and he locked the door before I could get it open. I waited outside the door, tapping my foot impatiently. I asked him nicely to come out, please.

"Only if you promise not to hurt me," he laughed. I crossed my heart and he opened the door.

He didn't have a foot on the ground before I pounced on him. "Don't you ever do that to me again!" I cried. He tried climbing back into his truck again.

"I'm sorry. I'm sorry," he said. He picked me up and hugged me, carrying me for a few steps before setting me back down. "I forgot your number, that's the only reason I didn't call. I'm sorry," he said, more gently this time.

"Just don't let it happen again," I laughed, exhilarating in being near him once more. We kissed, slowly, then went into the house.

My mother had just started supper and invited him to eat with us. "It's Saturday, so we're having hot dogs. Nothing fancy, but you're welcome to stay." She said it so cheerily and welcoming, I hoped he would notice the change in her.

He agreed, to my surprise, and took off his jacket. There was nothing special about the meal itself. We were sitting around the table talking, relaxed, friendly, and accepted. I looked from mother to father to boyfriend, and thought they were all amazing. At last, my mother understood. She knew what it was like to be in love. She spoke to him with a sociable tone, cracked some jokes at my expense, and looked at me through new eyes. Maybe she had a weakness after all. That thought was beyond belief.

Incredibly, he sincerely looked like he was having a good time. We had finished eating and I cleared the table. I wondered how he could concentrate on the conversation when he was watching my every move. I didn't know about him, but I wanted to be alone in his arms.

I excused myself and went into my room,

under the ruse that I was getting him the letter I had written him. I grabbed a piece of paper and scribbled 'Get me out of here, I don't care where, but I need a hug.' I slipped it into the letter, but only partially folded it so he could see the note, and handed it to him. He looked down briefly and set the letter aside. I began to think my subterfuge hadn't worked. He finished the point he was making to my dad, then said he had to buy a birthday present for his brother. He turned toward me and winked, asking me sweetly if I would like to go along with him.

My mother asked something about why he needed a woman's opinion for his brother's present, but we pretended not to hear as we closed the door behind us.

We drove to the local department store, looked around for a bit because he wanted to 'check the place out', then drove to a darker spot.

I asked him if he had a good time at the wedding. He smiled his smile . "Other than that," I clarified. I knew he was thinking about that damned garter. I was beginning to wish I had asked him to take me home when we were having that argument. 'After what I put him through to get permission for me to go, that would have been really rotten of me,' I thought to myself.

I had made him ask my parents for permission to take me to the wedding. He had just met them and I wasn't sure if Mom would let me go that far away on a 'date'. I also knew she wouldn't say no in front of him. She would say she would have to think about it, then give me her answer later.

We walked into the house and he backed up against the refrigerator. I was moving to stand next to Mom, but he said something like, "Oh, sure. Desert me!" I grabbed his hand and squeezed for strength.

He asked, "One of my friends is getting married next weekend and I would like to know if I could take your daughter?" He was so brave for someone looking down the gauntlet.

Mom said she didn't see any problem with it but he would have to ask my dad. I saw him shake himself. Most men respect, if not fear, their girlfriend's fathers. What he didn't know was, Dad was the easy one. He repeated the question to my father, who immediately saw the chance to make a joke.

"Yes, you can. But do you really want to?"

He took the question seriously at first, then laughed right along with him. I smiled at him my most radiant smile. He looked at me, trying to look mean, then gave up and let out a sigh of relief, 'whew'. Remembering this scene, I couldn't stop myself from wondering if a similar conversation was going to take place, only with a different question.

We had stayed on the subject of marriage, sitting there in the parking lot. I had only wanted to know if the bride and groom had a good time on their honeymoon, but this was a topic of conversation we couldn't seem to bypass. We started talking about how we would like to have our own weddings. Cautiously, testing the waters, each not wanting to say something to spook the other.

It started with individual weddings. Such as, "When I get married, I would like to have..." But he slipped up and said, "When we get married, I mean, *I* get married—" It wasn't much of a slip, it was what we both were thinking.

He stopped suddenly and looked out the window. My impulses took over and I pounced on the 'mistake'. "We? Are you thinking about it?"

I watched him fighting with himself in the half-lit truck. "Of course I have been thinking about it," he sighed. It was frightening to watch him purposefully not look at me. I knew he was waiting for me to say something. This was the conversation we both wanted to have. This was where we were. 'Now is the time.' I encouraged myself. 'Say something. Now! Tell him! Be Honest! He is right there, just reach out to him!'

What were the words to say? How do I keep this from becoming a total disaster if I say the wrong thing? Do I say 'I have been thinking about it too'? Is he going to believe what I say? Would he keep his promise to understand if I told him this? Why couldn't I admit to him that this was all I had managed to think about recently? 'Because you are terrified of the wrong reaction,' I answered myself.

I pictured myself reaching my hand out to put on his shoulder and saying, "I feel like I've known you all my life. I have been thinking about spending the rest of it with you since that day at the beach." He would turn to me and say, "Really? I thought we were just having fun. When you stop being fun, I'll stop coming up," and laugh at me, not with me, *at* me. That would be the wrong reaction.

I argued with myself yet again. 'You can't fake the emotion in his eyes. You know he loves you. Trust in that love. Where he leads, you will follow, remember? This is what you want. It is here, in your grasp, now!'

I couldn't say the words, so I wimped out. I decided to try to blow the whole thing off, like the whole idea of our ever getting married was ridiculous.

"I'm glad you fixed that," I said in the most negative tone I could muster. "I wouldn't want you to get the wrong idea."

"What wrong idea?" he asked, totally confused now.

"That I would marry you," I quipped back, still trying to keep up the act.

"What makes you think I would have, or ever will, ask you?" he teased, his eyes dancing.

I knew he was feeling better, but that last

remark was a little more than what was called for. I knew he was just joking with me, trying to get me going like he always did and I shouldn't give him the satisfaction, but that question really hurt.

I turned to him and forced a laugh. This exchange had gone too far already.

"What makes you think I want you to?" I sniped back.

He looked at me with total shock. His eyes changed from lighthearted to alarmed. "Well," he said, looking back out the window.

We were right back where we started from. I had hurt him. That was never my intention. His statement had been more than was called for, but mine was worse. I had purposely hurt him.

"I'm sorry," I said.

"Sorry for what?" he asked, still not looking at me. "For being honest?"

"I wasn't honest. I wanted to make you feel the way you made me feel when you asked me the same question." I needed him to hold me and tell me everything was all right, but only if everything really was all right. Would now be a good time to tell him what I couldn't tell him before: that I wanted his proposal?

"It feels pretty lousy," he said, attempting a smile.

"I know. I just got so mad. You hurt me and I wanted to hurt you. I never meant for it to go this far." I reached over and touched his arm where he had it draped over the steering wheel.

At last he turned and looked at me. I could see he was still hurting, but a different kind of hurt. He was tormented inside that he had caused me to feel any pain at all. He pulled me into his arms and kissed me. He was about to apologize, but I covered his lips with mine to silence him. I didn't need to hear a thing. No explanation, no apology, not even a promise that he wouldn't do it again. All I needed was him.

We let that topic fall to the wayside and I managed to bring up another that we had so far successfully avoided. I happened to mention I had talked to my aunt the past week. Remembering them, he asked how they were doing.

"They're both doing fine, and so are the children. Although, my aunt is still surprised that we are still seeing each other."

"Why? Didn't she think we would?"

"I think she knew we would for a while, but I don't think anyone would believe that we have fallen in love," I snuggled closer to him. "She says our age difference will come between us."

And that is where I stopped. He leaned back against his door and was looking out the window again. 'Damn,' I cursed myself. 'Don't you know when to shut up? And the things you should say, you don't!'

I sat there, letting him work this out for himself. I had butted in before and regretted it. This was something we both had to deal with in our own way.

"Your aunt and mother both bring up valid points. I will always be eight years older than you. We can never change that."

"I know, we can't pretend the problem doesn't exist, either," I started. Now I had the courage I needed only a little while before. I started to tell him my news from the past week: the understanding with my mother, the negotiated curfew, the application to college, everything.

"As long as you know," he said with

finality. He looked out the window and quickly back at me again. "Is that a cop that just drove in there?" he asked, pointing to the building across the street from where we sat.

"Yes," I said. "That's the sheriff's office building, or some law enforcement, I'm not sure which."

He looked at me with disbelief. "Do you mean to tell me we have been making out across the street from a cop house?"

"Yes," I said, loving the look on his face. "I thought this was pretty ingenious. They would never look for us right under their noses—"

I never finished what I was going to say because he started the truck and was pulling onto the road. "I don't believe you!" he laughed. He drove away like a crazy man trying to put as much distance between us and the station.

"Is there a place we can be alone without cops?" he asked after driving around town and 'testing' a few parking lots. He would pull in, park the truck, pull me into his arms, kiss me, then start the truck again after saying, "Nope, this one doesn't feel right either."

I gave him directions to a secluded spot I had passed two weeks earlier. A dirt fishing road curved away from the main road and ended under a bridge from the road above in a big circle. We were completely hidden.

"This is a pretty secluded spot," he said, looking around. "People come down here to fish?"

"Among other things," I hinted. I slid across the seat and hung his arm around me.

"Like what?" he kidded. I gave him a look of surprise not believing he could be that dense, but he only laughed and hugged me closer. "You brought me here to take advantage of me, didn't you?"

"You wanted secluded and alone," I replied, moving to pull away to my side of the truck.

He tightened his arm around me, preventing that, and tipped my face up to his. I wrapped my arms around his neck and surrendered. I knew he wanted to do more than kiss. I wanted him to make love to me and I wanted to make love to him.

His lips wandered down my neck, but didn't stop at my collar like always. He pushed my jacket back off my shoulders and down my arms to continue his exploration. He kissed his way around the neckline of my blouse and assaulted my ear on the other side.

He slid his hands from around me to caress up and down my sides. He reached for the buttons on my blouse and I leaned back to give him easier access. He tipped my head back to look into my eyes for just an instant before he dipped his head to kiss each inch of skin at it was exposed.

I trembled all over. My hands were shaking as I pushed him back to take off his jacket. I slipped my hands under his shirt and felt his heart pounding. I pushed his shirt over his head and ran my hands over his bare chest. I leaned over him where he lay against the door of the truck and let my lips follow my hands in their investigation of his upper body.

He groaned and pushed me backwards on the seat so now I was the one laying against my door. He finished unbuttoning my blouse and pushed it off my shoulders. He feasted his eyes on my breasts and looked up at me with undeniable hunger in his eyes.

"God, you are so beautiful," he whispered

against my neck. He looked into my eyes intently, looking for any sign of hesitation, before he took my lips once more. He ran his tongue across my cheek to my ear like he had so many times before, but this time he followed my collar bone down to the base of my neck. He reached up with one hand to cup a breast while he reached around with his other to push me up to meet his lips.

I needed no urging. I arched my back and pushed one hand against his head to somehow bring him closer. His mouth was making my nerves dance. His hot breath did little but make my skin burn more. He finished his gentle assault of my breasts and followed his hand down to where it rested above my navel.

I couldn't lie there any longer. I murmured something about turn-about being fair play and pushed him backwards until he was lying on the seat. Starting at his knees, I ran my hands up his pants, over his abdomen, stopping only long enough to tug playfully at the hair on his chest, then encircled them around his neck. I pressed myself along the length of him and he moaned as he ran his fingers lightly up my spine from the waist of my jeans to entwine themselves in my hair. He slanted my head and ravaged my mouth.

I felt so helpless. I loved him so much. He was kissing me so hard it almost hurt. It was exquisite. The gentle torture he was putting me through. I instinctively moved my hips against him and he groaned. I had wanted to relieve the pressure I found building there, but only succeeded in feeding the fire. He ground his mouth so hard against mine I cried out. I couldn't have cooled things down any faster if I had thrown a bucket of ice water on him.

He sat up instantly and said, "I knew I would hurt you." He pulled me close again and began stroking my hair gently as he apologized over and over. When I tried to explain that he hadn't really hurt me, he looked around at where we were.

"We can't do this. Not here, anyways." I looked up at him with tears in my eyes when he said the first, the he quickly amended it with his last remark.

"Look at me," he said, forcing me to look into his eyes. Even though he had said the right words, I had started to cry. I was picturing what was going through his mind at that time.

'He must think I'm a tramp,' I said to myself. That thought only made me cry harder. I buried my head in his shoulder and shivered. He must have thought I was cold because he put my shirt back over my shoulders and buttoned it up.

He pulled me back into his arms after he hung my jacket back around me. I never stopped crying through the whole process and he was at his wits-end to figure out why.

"Come on, honey. What's the matter?" he asked, gently kissing my forehead. I shook my head to say nothing was wrong, but he gave me the look that meant he wanted to know, and know now.

"I know what you must be thinking of me right now, and I don't want you to think that way about me," I sniffed as an answer.

"Is that why you're so upset? That I had the wrong idea?"

He sounded so surprised. Had the idea never occurred to him that I may have very little self-esteem at that time?

"Yes." I pulled out of his arms to sit alone on the other side of the truck. "If you didn't want to make love to me, you should have just said so and not made up some excuse about hurting me."

He followed me across the seat and looked at me with disbelief. "I do want to make love to you, but not here," he said, waving a hand around the truck. "If I... no... *When* I make love to you, it is going to be in a bed, and take all night long, not in the front seat of my truck."

It was my turn to look surprised. I thought he would have started the truck and taken me directly home. Wait, what did he call me?

"Do you know what you called me?" I needed confirmation.

"What?" he said, looking around like something in the truck would give him a clue.

"You called me 'honey'!" I said the words so forcefully that I wanted to reach into his memory to kick it into action.

"Oh, that," he said. "For a minute there, I thought I had moaned the wrong name," he kidded. I laughed right along with him until I noticed he was looking at me with my look.

"Honey, I love you," he said, pulling me back into his arms.

We whispered the phrase over and over, holding one another, each lost in their own thoughts. He turned away, looking out over the river with his arm around me like when we first met. When he turned back he noticed the clock on the dashboard. "Let's get you home early for a change," he said, starting the engine.

I had the same thought earlier in the day and set the alarm on my watch. It sounded as we made the turn into my driveway.

He noticed me turning if off and said, "I ought to buy you another watch for Christmas so you wouldn't have to wear that damn thing anymore."

"Oh, I've already got your present," I announced, proud of the fact that I was ahead of the game.

"How do you know we will still be together then?" he asked.

I wasn't sure if he was serious or not, or if he was trying to get a rise out of me like always. As a rule, I was trying to not fall into those traps by answering joke questions with serious answers, but this one made me feel suddenly scared and excited at the same time. Scared because I didn't want him to say we wouldn't, and excited because I wanted him to say we would.

"Is there a possibility we won't be?" I asked shakily. 'Don't do this to me now,' I prayed. 'I could handle this a few weeks ago. Please, not now.'

"There's always a possibility, but I have no other plans for that particular holiday," he joked. The look he gave me when he parked the truck put my fears to rest, crisis averted. We kissed goodnight, I wished him a safe drive home, then walked into the house at five minutes to eleven.

My mother looked at the clock and made an applauding gesture. I stuck my tongue out at her and said, "You didn't think we could do it, did you?" Leaving her smiling, I headed for bed.

Chapter Twelve

The next Thursday afternoon I received a call from a neighbor. She and her older daughter wanted to go Christmas shopping and could I watch her three younger children the next day. 'Friday is the only day I get to see him, but I need the money,' I argued with myself. My good sense took over and I accepted. He usually doesn't show up until around six, and my neighbor promised she would be back by then.

The plan was that I would get off the bus with the kids at their house and stay until their mother and sister got home. The children didn't really need babysitting, only someone to handle a serious emergency if one should arise. The bus turned the corner by my house and his truck was in the driveway.

'What is it with him?' I asked myself. 'He usually has a sixth sense about these things.' I got off the bus, after telling the kids I would be at their house in ten minutes and not to leave until I got there, and walked up the driveway. 'I can't blame him for coming early,' I said as I made the short truck from road to house. 'He didn't know I had a job this afternoon.'

I opened the door that led into the garage and three people looked up at me in guilty surprise. My mother, my father, and he all turned when I said hello.

"I thought you were getting off the bus at the neighbor's," Mom said.

"I was going to, but I wanted to know why he showed up so early," I said, looking up at him. He turned that smile on me and I almost melted into the floor.

"I thought I would come early because I have to leave early," he said.

He took one look at my expression and added, "It's not that bad, I can stay for a little while. I want to go hunting tomorrow and need a good nights sleep so I can get up in the morning."

'Oh, is that all,' I said to myself. I didn't give it another thought until we were driving to my neighbor's house. You know that feeling you get when you walk into a room and know the people were talking about you? That feeling followed me all the way down the road. Before we got out of the truck, I asked him what he and my parents were talking about before I interrupted them.

"Wouldn't you like to know?" he joked.

"Yes, I would," I said flatly, absolutely, positively, dead serious.

He looked at me with a surprised expression to answer the worried one I had on my face. He got out of the truck and held his hand out to help me across the seat to get out his side. "It's nothing to be worried about," he assured me. He had always been honest with me, brutally at times, so I had no reason to doubt him this time. I made a mental note to revisit the question another time.

The three children had waited until I got there before they scattered in less than five minutes. "This should be easy money," I said to him.

"You just let them run around like that?" he asked.

"You forget, I grew up here. I know everyone on this road and I know them well enough to know that none of them have any qualms about sending them straight home if they get into trouble."

"O.k.," he said. "I just don't want you to get fired from this job," he laughed.

"I can't get fired from this job," I laughed

back.

Two hours flew by. My neighbor returned home right at six o'clock like she said she would, paid me, and we got in the truck to go back to my house.

Once there, I asked him into the house for bit, hoping to get him to change his mind about leaving. My mother had gone somewhere and my father was cooking his own supper when we entered the kitchen. I offered to make both men supper, but my father said he could do it himself and my boyfriend reminded me that he had to get going.

At a few minutes past six, he asked me to walk him out to his truck. He took my hand and walked very slowly out the kitchen door, down the steps to the garage, then out into the driveway. He leaned back against the truck and put both warm hands on my hips. I slid my hands up his arms, loving the feel of the muscles beneath, and laid them on his shoulders.

He knew me well enough to know I had something on my mind when I didn't look at him. He leaned over and looked up at me from his bent over position and smiled his goofy smile. I couldn't help but laugh when his glasses slipped off and landed on the gravel of the driveway.

"Are they broken?" I asked as he picked them up.

"No, they're all right. But are you?" he asked, looking at me concerned.

"Yes, I just don't want you to go," I said. There was nothing else to say. I didn't want him to go and that was what was bothering me. 'Honesty at all costs,' I thought.

I caught the feeling something was bothering him. I was standing in his arms, yet he was miles away.

"I don't want to go, either. But I made a promise to go hunting with this guy tomorrow, and I've got to go," he assured me.

It's true I didn't want him to go, but I would rather have him keep his word. This sounds very old fashioned in these days and times, but if he wouldn't keep his word to a friend, was I sure he would keep it to me? I already knew the answer to that and I knew he had to go.

"I'll see you next weekend?" I asked, looking for just a little reassurance.

"I'll see," he said vaguely. He wouldn't look me in the eyes. I tried to turn his face towards mine, but he closed his eyes and kissed me instead. I kissed him back, but with no feeling.

"If you keep kissing me like that, I won't come next week," he threatened lightly. He was kidding at a time like this! That made me so mad, I wanted to...I don't know what I wanted to do.

"I didn't know that you seeing me depended on my performance the week before!" I snapped.

He realized his mistake and crushed me into his arms, stroking my hair. "Honey, I don't have much more time. Can we just make the most of it?" He wanted me to forget and hold him. He was sorry he had to go, but really did want to make what little time we had count. 'Time is all there is, make it count,' I remembered him saying when he gave me his ring.

I was drowning in the tidal wave of emotions churning inside of me. A single one never surfaced long enough for me concentrate on it. I didn't know where to look or what to say or how to act.

"Well, if you've got to go, you've got to

go," I said. I stood on my toes and kissed his cheek. He reached to put his arms around me, but I took a step back.

He dropped his hands to his sides and leaned back against the truck, defeated. "I'm sorry," he sighed, looking down. He looked so tired and defenseless. I wanted to put my arms around him and hold him close and apologize. I wanted to tell him that I would take as little or as much time as he could give me. I wanted to tell him I loved him.

I started to walk away towards the house and I heard him call after me, "I'm sorry!"

I snapped. It was all too much for me to bear. "I know, you just have to go kill those dear!" I shouted. I slammed the door behind me and started to primly march up the stairs to the house, then I looked out the window. I saw him still standing beside his truck, hand on the door, watching me walk up the stairs.

I stopped mid-step. 'Go now!' I yelled at myself. 'Run to him, throw your arms around him and tell him everything you wanted to. Do not let him leave like this! Dammit, stop thinking and move, Now!'

I watched him get in his truck and drive
away.

Chapter Thirteen

I received no letter from him that week, even though I had written him several. In each, I apologized for saying what I did and not understanding when he asked me to. Thursday night rolled around and I didn't get my usual call. We had made arrangements to meet in front of the school that Friday.

It was Halloween. My parents were going away for the weekend and I was staying with a sister who lived right in town. We had driven by her house so he would know where to go the last Saturday he had been up. He insisted he would forget, so I asked him to meet me in front of the school on the main street and I would show him the way. It sounded like a good plan at the time.

I walked to my sister's house after school, then, when he was supposed to meet me, I walked back to the school. I waited for three hours for him to show up. I walked home in the dark.

My sister and her husband were going to their hunting camp when I got back. They asked if I wanted to come, but I declined. If he had to work late again, I said, I wanted to be there if he

265

remembered which house it was. They said o.k. and started off. Alone in the house, I waited until two-thirty before going to bed.

The next day, a friend of theirs stopped by to pick up something they needed at camp and asked if I wanted a ride up. I declined again, saying that he might have to work on a Saturday like before and he would stop by that night. I went to bed at three o'clock that morning.

Sunday rolled around and I still hadn't heard from him. I had sent him my sister's phone number, so he couldn't say he had left it at home, when he was home already. I slept all day Sunday and woke when my sister and her husband came home. She wanted to know all about my date, having heard so much about him. Did we enjoy not having a curfew and having the house all to ourselves?

"There's nothing to tell," I stated.

She said something like, "I remember the last time I was stood up," and looked at her husband. He walked out of the room whistling innocently.

'Have I really been stood up?' I asked

myself. Saying it that way sounded so demeaning, when there had to be a perfectly logical explanation.

It was evening, around eight o'clock when I asked my sister's permission to use the phone to call him. He was home all right. Hearing his voice made me feel better; then my brain took over and I started asking questions. Apparently his work office had called and needed him to work in their lab that afternoon. He was almost home by the time I had gotten out of school. I wondered why he hadn't called to let me know, but he never really answered that question. He changed the subject to tell me about his new car he had picked up over the weekend. I asked him about it and he said, "You remember. I showed it to you. The 'forty-nine Cady in—"

He broke off his sentence, realizing his mistake. He had showed me the car. It was in a lot being sold in my town. He had noticed it one evening and pulled over to take a closer look. He asked me to write the number down for him so he could get more information. I remember the comment I had made about it. "That much? Do you have that kind of money?"

He winked at me and nodded, "I have that kind of money."

'He had driven up here to pick up a car, and not to see me,' I repeated to myself, staggered. When I asked him why, he said he couldn't remember where the house was and his father was with him. I couldn't believe what I was hearing. I asked if I would see him the next weekend, or at the very least get a letter from him. He said I might, laughingly. I had enough of that conversation. I said a quick goodbye and hung up.

I did get a letter from him the next week. Or rather, half a letter. I noticed immediately he didn't sign it 'love'. He basically scribbled his name on the bottom like he usually did. He did put a P.S. at the bottom: 'Your watch wasn't reading the same time as mine.'

One of the many coincidences in our relationship was that our watches always read the same time, right down to the second. It could have been a big coincidence, like I said, but we took it as a good omen. Now he was saying our time wasn't right.

I wrote him a few more letters, but after

getting no response, I had to think more into this than I had allowed myself before. The last stamp I asked my mother for prompted a long-contained reaction by her. She took me by the hand and led me into the living room and sat me down on the couch.

"I can't take you like this anymore," she started.

"Mom, I really don't want to get into this with you." I made a move to get up.

"Sit down," she said firmly. "We need to discuss this like two rational adults. Isn't that what you want from me? Look at you like the adult you have become?" When I nodded, she continued, "You will always be my little girl, no matter if you are sixteen or thirty-six. You are hurting and a mother can't stand it when her child is in pain."

I just burst into tears, emotionally spent. I had kept everything inside not wanting to bother anyone with my nonsense. Here before me was my mother, extending kindness and understanding for what she saw me going through. I hadn't hid it as well as I thought I had, I guess.

"What is going on with you two?" she

asked, handing me a tissue. "You didn't want him to go hunting?" she tried.

I laughed at that. Now that I was actually talking to my mother, I didn't know where to begin.

"It is so much more than that, Mom. We made a promise that we could tell each other anything in the world and we would understand. And I didn't."

"That's a pretty big promise," she exclaimed.

I smiled and continued, "We also made a promise that time was precious and to make it count. And I didn't. Stupid, Stupid, Stupid!"

"You came in the house and cried for an hour," she finished. At my questioning look she added, "Yes, I know. Your father told me all about it when I got home. I went in to check on you and you were sleeping. Did you cry yourself to sleep that night?"

"I think so," was all I could manage. I looked back into the file system of my memory under 'things to revisit' and asked the question which answer I was dying to have. "What did you three talk about that day before I got home?"

"I don't remember the exact words," she replied. "Did you ask him? What did he say?"

"He laughed and told me it was nothing I needed to worry about."

"That pretty much covers it," she agreed. Was I never going to get a straight answer?

"So, what do you think he is doing now?" she covered the lull in the discussion.

I coughed, choking on my own thoughts. "I know exactly what he is doing."

"And what is that?" she asked.

"He is driving himself crazy thinking, just like I am," I answered.

"And what is he thinking?" she pushed. She was going to make me say this. Any lawyer will tell you never to ask a question you don't already know the answer to.

"He's wondering if I'm worth loving," I whispered.

"I wouldn't say it like that!" she exclaimed. "You are definitely 'worth' loving," she patted my leg.

"Am I worth all the trouble it will mean to keep seeing me?" I amended.

"Well, if you're going to be trouble, I wouldn't want to see you either," she scoffed.

"Worth all the difficulty, then," I was exasperated. I felt like she was backing me purposely into a corner. She knew me well enough to know I would come out swinging.

"Are you?" she asked, lifting her chin.

"Yes!" I hollered back.

She hugged me tightly. "I raised all my girls to know there own worth. I'm glad to see you haven't lost yours."

We both took a deep breath before I brought up something she had said in passing a few weeks ago. She had made a comment that I made him do 'all the work' in the relationship. He had to drive to see me, he paid for everything, he spent money on pay phones to call me, and the fact that he drove to get me and take me home in one day when we went to the wedding confounded her.

"After all, I do make him do all the work in this relationship," I joked. Honesty time, "He wanted me to come down the Friday night before the wedding so I could go to the rehearsal dinner with him, and he wouldn't have to drive so much. I told him there was no way you would go for that."

"You're right," she nodded. "We had only just met him then. We didn't know what kind of man he was or if we could trust him or you."

"You see, that's what he wants," I tried to say, fighting for the words. "That's what he is doing right now. He goes out with his friends, looks around, and is still alone."

"It's not my responsibility to make it easier for him to see you," she said, reverting back to her old self for minute.

"Remember, Mom, adult?" I giggled. She rolled her eyes. "He tells me he goes out on weekends with his friends. His favorite place needs proof of age to get in the door. He's going to wait five years until I can go with him? It's like, his hands are tied from loving me and having the relationship he really wants to have with me" At her disapproving look I knew I had to make my point. "It's not the drinking. That's an attractive picture: my girlfriend comes to see me, gets drunk, and throws up in the bathroom. Yeah, I want him to see me do that." She laughed at my example. "It's the experience. Instead of talking *about* me, he wants to be able to put his arm around me and have me there, with him. God knows what his friends say. They probably pick on him mercilessly."

I stopped to take a breath, I was talking so fast. She listened to what I said, not interrupting, but letting me rant. "I'm sure the phrase 'cradle-robber' has been bandied about. 'He couldn't bring his girlfriend, it's a school night'; and 'Can't you find someone your own age'; and all the comments that go along with that. I made an ass out of myself at that wedding."

"Friends can be a big influence," is all she said.

"They don't know me, and I will never get a fair shot for them to get to know me." I said bitterly. "Everything I do is prefaced by 'sixteen'. And I'm stuck up here!!"

"I know you are frustrated, but it's not up to you. It's up to him to tell his friends either that they are right, or to shut-up."

"He's told me so many things he would like to do with me," I stopped, realizing the double meaning in that statement. She waved her hand, motioning me to go on. "He wants me to get to know his family and friends. He wants to kiss me at midnight on New Year's and all the great stuff two people like us should be able to do. And I go and blow it. I acted like a spoiled child. Like he couldn't do something without my permission, like…" I trailed off.

"Like buy a house?" she asked. That stopped my tirade short. "Does he know all that you have done in the past three short months? You're going to college next year? You're buying a car? All, I suspect, because of him. Before you go beating yourself up too much, let's be fair and spread the blame around a little."

"No, I haven't told him that yet. That is a face-to-face conversation. I want to see the look in his eyes when I do. Along with what he and his mother talked about."

"Talked about what?" she asked, confused.

"He wrote in a letter that he had a talk with his mom the same weekend Dad had sprung his message on us before we went to Canada. He said it was too much to write," I laughed. "We haven't had a chance to do much talking in a while," I sighed.

"How do you think that went?"

"I don't have the vaguest idea. There are only two choices, realistically. She either tried to talk him out of seeing me, or into seeing me." At least I was honest. Time for another long awaited answer.

"I know you didn't like him at first. Was it the age? Did you think I would change myself to fit him? Did you think he wouldn't 'let' me go to college? Don't you think I can have it all? Marriage, career and family?" I prattled on questions.

"The only thing I didn't like about him when I first met him was his age. He has proven himself to be quite wonderful. I had hoped you wouldn't change for him, and I'm thrilled to see you didn't. And he will keep you in college, you have someone to love and be proud of you now, not just me. Can you have it all?" she shook her head and grinned. "You are just determined and smart enough, you won't stop until you do."

"Are you worried about the marriage part?" I asked plainly.

"Well, yes, if you must know," she

answered, surprised. "I don't want you to think being married is easy. Right now, all you see are sunshine and roses."

"You don't think I know how hard it could be to make a marriage work? You don't think I am looking at things clearly? It's hard enough to have a good marriage, and to top it off, let's throw in all the things we have going against us. I see good marriages *all* around me: yours and dad's, my brother next door, how many sisters do I have?" I paused as she laughed. "Tell me, what haven't I thought of? Money? Health Insurance? Mortgage rates? My college financial aid? Compromising? Intimacy? Children? Will we have the ceremony up here or down there? How high will his auto insurance go up when he adds me to his policy? You tell me, what haven't I thought of?"

She sat there, shocked. "O.k., so maybe you have thought about this more than a little. I wish we could have talked like this a while ago," she admitted. There was more to that statement than she was letting on. "Have you told him all this?" she asked again.

"Arrgh," I grunted in frustration. "We were

there. It was the topic of conversation. He dropped a hint, sat there waiting for my reply. I couldn't get the words out. I sat there screaming at myself: Tell him, tell him, tell him. Buy Boardwalk!"

I was so upset with myself I couldn't sit still anymore. I had jumped up and started pacing back and forth to relieve my pent up anger. My mother burst out laughing.

"Why in the world didn't you just say so?" she managed between gales of laughter.

I sat back down, spent. "I don't think I could have handled the rejection."

If anything could have sobered my mother, that was the one thing that did.

"Are you going to write him all the things you haven't told him yet? Maybe that will help him with his decision."

"I want him to *want* to love me. I don't want him to love me because I made it easier for him. I made these plans because I want us to be together, not because I thought it would be a good way to keep him. How can I make you understand?"

"Oh, I get it," she nodded. "We'll have to

talk about New Year's Eve, though," she hinted.

"So, you're o.k. with us? He and I?" I asked, desperate for some sign of acknowledgement.

She took her time, and a big deep breath, before she answered me. "You're my last child, my baby. It is hard to think of having to let you go. I was only hoping I could keep you for a little while yet." Her eyes welled up with tears.

"Don't you think he will take good care of me?" I wanted to set her fears aside.

"I have never seen another man look at any woman the way he looks at you," she vowed.

"What if he doesn't come back?" I said, almost in tears again.

Pulling herself together, she said, "Then you will have had your first broken heart."

"Gee, thanks!" I couldn't contain my sarcasm, then added seriously. "What if he does?"

She took my face in her hands, emphasizing her words, "Then, love him forever."

I couldn't stop the tears from rolling down my cheeks at her advice.

She grabbed some more tissue and handed it

to me. "Your eyes are far too beautiful to ever be filled with tears."

I completely forgot about the stamp I had wanted.

It had been five weeks since I had last seen or heard from him. I had written him one final letter. I didn't think I would have the courage to issue an ultimatum, but I told him I couldn't live in this limbo any longer. If he wanted his ring back and never see me again, all he had to do was say so. As much as it would hurt to say goodbye, there was very little I could do if that is what he wanted.

Near the end of the week, I did get a letter from him. This was like no other letter I had ever read. It wasn't cold or demanding, neither was it loving or promising. It was informational and impersonal. It was the type of letter one would get addressed to 'Dear Sir'.

He had the first week of December off, it said, and he wanted to see me one of those days, let him know which.

I was planning to spend the Thanksgiving

vacation with my aunt. I missed her and my uncle and the children. If anyone could help me, she could.

One of her first questions was how we were doing. I looked at her and said, "I don't know, I haven't seen him in six weeks."

"How come?" she asked with obvious sympathy.

"I don't know. He said he wanted to see me sometime next week. I'm supposed to let him know which day."

"Have you?" she asked.

"No, not yet. I was hoping you would let me call him."

"Sure," she said. "I hope everything is all right between you tow. He is such a nice guy, this doesn't sound like him at all."

"I hope everything is all right, too" I sniffed, very near tears.

This telephone conversation wasn't very different from his letter. The usual hello's and how are you's. He said he was going to Canada Tuesday morning and that he would like to stop and see me on the way home. I told him that would be fine.

We both just hung up.

'Fine,' I berated myself. 'You couldn't have said something different than fine?'

I forced myself to come to grips with the decision I had to make. I would accept whatever he said. It was a difficult concept to grapple with, but I found it much easier to live with myself for the next few days until Tuesday came.

All day I answered questions about him. I said, 'I'm seeing him tonight,' so many times, I should have made a recording.

It started snowing early in the afternoon, those big fluffy flakes that lazily drift down and cover everything. I had given up all hope of seeing him, thinking the weather would keep him from coming. I had barely finished the dishes when I got home from school when I saw lights in the driveway.

"He's here," Mom said, quietly and cautiously. She didn't think he would come, either.

I asked her for some privacy so we could talk, then opened the door. My mother asked him about the weather, then excused herself to help my father in the basement where he was working.

I offered him a seat in the living room, then sat beside him. I wanted to sit in his lap and wrap my arms around him. I wanted to tell him I loved him and I always would. Instead, I sat a reasonable distance away.

Neither of us knew where to start. Or maybe it was where to end. I noticed the minute I opened the door he wasn't wearing his key necklace. He usually wore it proudly displayed on the outside of whatever shirt he was wearing. Now it was gone.

I had written down a few questions for him throughout the day do I wouldn't forget them. I suggested he read them, and he opened his hands to show he would. I retrieved them from my book bag and gave them to him. He read them through, then asked for a pen. It would have been romantic, him writing his answers to me, but I knew he was only doing it because he couldn't say the words out loud. Reading his answers, I knew what he was getting at. Bringing myself to accept it was harder than I ever imagined, pre-made decision or not.

I looked up when Mom came back into the house. She looked at my face and knew what was going on. He looked up quickly, saw the look on her face, and immediately looked back down, almost guiltily.

"I'm not staying, I just have to go to the bathroom," she said on her way through the house.

"You don't have to go, you know," he said. "We aren't kicking you out or anything, are we?"

"No, but I'm under orders from my daughter," she said on her way back out.

He turned to me with disbelief on his face. "You kicked your own mother out?"

"I didn't kick her anywhere. I asked her for a little privacy so we could talk."

He nodded to indicate he understood and handed me the paper back. I wrote one more question on the folded side. 'So, what's next? Do you want to stay here for diner or ride around and try your luck in town? We could get really desperate and go to a volleyball game. You really don't want to spend the rest of the evening with Mom and Dad, do you?'

After visiting with them for a few minutes after they came in from their work, he asked me where the volleyball game was. We got in his truck and I gave him directions to the school. He knew where it was, but the lack of conversation was eerie.

I leaned over, like I always had, to hold his hand, but this time was different. He held my hand, but not tightly. His fingers didn't intertwine comfortably with mine, but hung limply. I let go and leaned back against the door of the truck. When he asked me why I let go, I said something about my hands being cold and not wanting to make his cold as well. 'I'm not the one letting go,' I said to him in my thoughts.

It only took him a few minutes of the game to announce he had enough and wanted to go. I followed him out to the truck. He got in on his side and unlocked the door from the latch on the inside. There was another oddity. He always unlocked my door first and I would unlock his from the inside. Passing under a street light driving to wherever we were going to end up, I noticed the 'I love you' had been washed off the window.

We drove to the parking lot we had spent a lot of time in. He pulled over to a deserted section with no street lights and cut the engine. He sat there, gripping the steering wheel, staring out the window like I'd watched him do plenty of times before when he was trying to begin a subject and didn't know how to. And when he did, it was the subject I had dreaded for weeks.

"I want to talk to you about something," he said, still not looking at me.

"And that would be?" I asked

"I tried to give you and inkling earlier tonight, in the letter," he said, finally turning to me.

"No," I said. I knew what he was saying.

"Yes," he said. I looked away, out the window, or at a passing car, simply away from him.

"Why?" I asked, amazingly calm for knowing he was about to rip my heart out.

"A lot of reasons," he answered, calmly.

"It's my age, isn't it," I taunted. I was going to get at least one good reason out of him if I had to get him mad to do it.

"No, well, yes, I guess," he stammered.

"You don't even know why?" I asked, incredulously.

"I know why, I am just having a hard time putting it into words," he said. He had leaned towards me when he had said yes, but now he leaned back against his door.

"I know why," I said. I had no idea why, truthfully, but I was hoping I could bluff him into telling me. I had to hear it from his lips. "You don't love me anymore."

"No!" he said, bolting straight up in the seat. "You're wrong. I do love you. I love you very much, and I always will."

"Then why are you breaking up with me?" I cried. I couldn't stop the tears. I had been trying to be so brave about this, but all I wanted to do was go home, curl up and cry until I was dehydrated.

"I have to," he said, pulling me into his arms. "Don't you see that I have to?"

"Is there somebody else?" I nearly whispered.

"No, there is no one else," he assured me firmly.

"Then why?" I asked again, searching desperately for the answer I needed.

"I want to get married, buy a house, and start a family," he said, not looking at me.

"A year and a half. That's all you would have to wait and I could do that with you," I stated, giving one last effort to turn him around.

He looked me straight in the eyes and said, "I don't want to wait that long."

I was stunned. At last I had the answer I was searching for. I sometimes wish he had lied and said there was someone else. Another woman I could handle, there was no contest with time.

"Then I suppose you want this back?" I asked, taking off his ring and holding it out to him.

"Not right at the moment," he said.

"What the hell do you want from me?" I screamed, throwing his ring on the dashboard. His last comment made me blow a fuse. I pushed him away when he would have pulled me into his arms again and tried to open the door to run away.

"No," he said as he pulled me back into the truck and locked the door. He repeated my name over and over, trying to break the hysteria that had built inside me. He pulled me into his arms tenderly and held me, rocking me and stroking my hair as I cried.

"What do I want from you?" he repeated my question. "I want you to understand. That's what I want from you, understanding."

"Understand that you don't love me anymore?" I asked.

"I do love you, too much at times," he said, shaking his head to emphasize his statement. "I want you to understand why I have to do this."

Understanding? He actually wanted me to understand something I did not agree with. I couldn't begin to fathom his audacity to ask me to understand. 'How dare he?' I asked myself. 'Where you lead, I will follow. And this is where you lead me?' I didn't understand why he hadn't just written back and said he wanted to break up. I would have sent him his ring, no questions asked. Well, a few questions asked. But no, not him! He had to come up in person and humiliate me.

Then it hit me. He had come up. It would have been much easier to just write me to send him his ring. He wanted me to ask questions. He wanted to be the one to answer them; the best he could, anyway. He really did need me to try to see things from his point of view. I had been doing that for weeks; now, I had to accept them, not hoping for the best.

He wasn't trying to humiliate me. He was

treating me with respect, like he always had. And honoring what we had together by trying to give it's ending a smidge of dignity. How could I refuse him the very last request he would ever make of me?

"I'll try," I gave in, quietly. Too quietly because he asked me to repeat myself.

"I'm not sure I can understand, but I'm going to give it a try" I said, faking a brave smile.

He pulled me into his arms and squeezed so hard I had to ask him to let me go. I hadn't given him the secret of life or a cure for cancer, I wanted to keep my spine intact. He laughed with relief.

"Please, take me home," I asked coldly.

He leaned back in his seat again, sighing dejectedly.

"I'm not taking you anywhere," he ground out, "until we get through this."

"Get through what? I said I would try to understand, what more do you want?" I argued back. What more could there possibly be?

A deep sounding, fairly pleading voice came out of the darkness. "I don't want you to hate me."

"You can't have it both ways! You want it all, but nothing. You can't have everything, but end up with nothing. You don't want me to hate you, but you don't want me to love you. You can't have both!" I hollered.

"I didn't say I didn't want you to love me, I just said I didn't want you to hate me."

"I don't hate you. I couldn't ever hate you. I love you too much." It was my turn to lean back dejectedly. Neither of us could get what we wanted. It was so unfair. Why had God put us into each other's lives to just tear us apart again?

"I love you, too," he cried. He looked at me with tears in his eyes, helpless. He had only cried one other time in front of me, but under much different circumstances. He wanted me, to be with me, to love, to hold me and share with me, knowing how impossible that would be, he had no choice but to let me go. He loved me enough to hurt us both by doing what he thought was right.

We sat in silence, each enveloped with their own thoughts.

I don't know how we got there, or what was said to bring up the subject, but he ended up going through the drive-thru window at the McDonald's across the parking lot. He ordered a twenty-piece

McNuggets and every kind of sauce they had. He had never tried them before and decided it was time.

We drove back to the spot we were just at and started eating. He was making small talk about how many times he had gone to that fast-food place and couldn't believe he had never tried them. I was thinking about his tears and savory the last few moments I would have with him.

"Does it hurt?" I asked, thinking I would regret the answer.

"Yes," he said, taking another bite.

"Then, why do it?" I asked. Couldn't hurt to give it one last-ditch effort.

"I have to," he said simply, licking sauce off his fingers.

"I wish I had been born at least three years earlier," I said vainly, knowing full well that if anything were different, there was a good chance we never would have met in the first place.

"So do I!" he agreed. He looked heavenward, asking God the same question. "We have gone as far as we can realistically go with this relationship," he said.

I knew he was right. But at that particular

point of time, I didn't want to be realistic. I wanted my P.C. back.

"I wish we would have made love," I said.

"Boy, do I wish I had made love to you," he agreed fervently, finally turning to look at me again. He slid his arm around me and we leaned into each other.

"I have been writing a story about us," I said, waiting for his full attention before continuing. "It is all about our times together. It was supposed to end with us getting married, not breaking up. I do love happy endings," I joked.

He laughed too, then said, "You finish that story. You can end it anyway you want to. Just promise me you'll write it."

His request was so sincere, I could do nothing but say, "I promise."

"Besides," he laughed again, "I can't wait to get all those royalty checks."

I laughed with him this time. "Not if I don't mention any names, I said.

"I would like to see you try to write a book without names," he dared, looking at me intently.

"You just watch," I answered his challenge.

I was trying to catch the emotion in his eyes while he was still looking at me; but in the darkness of the truck, it was very hard.

He noticed what I was trying to do because his eyes changed immediately. "You're trying to read something," he said, turning away.

"I'm sorry," I said. "I didn't know what I saw there anyways. It looked like confusion, but I couldn't see in the dark."

"That's good," he laughed. He pulled me into his arms one last time before he started the truck to take me home.

We got back to my house around ten-thirty. I asked him to come in so I could give him his Christmas present. It had been delivered to school that morning and I had wrapped it that afternoon before he arrived.

He tried to talk me out of giving it to him, but I told him no one else would get the joke involved. He reluctantly followed me into the house. I went to the kitchen drawer where my mom kept her scissors and cut the yarn off his ring. I had wrapped it so carefully around it, I was surprised that it didn't take much effort to cut it off. 'Much like our relationship,' I though.

Mom saw me handing it back to him and asked, "You two are breaking up?"

I nodded my head as I walked past her to get his present from my room, leaving him alone to face my mother. She looked at him with surprise and something else I couldn't identify.

I laid his gift in front of him and put another on the counter. He slowly opened his, checking to see if anything was going to jump out at him. He pulled out a sweatshirt that said, "Kiiss mich! Ich spreche Deutsch!"

He read it, or tried to, then looked at me and said, "All right, smarty, now what does it say?"

"It's German. It says 'Kiss me! I speak German!' I told you no one else would get it but you," I laughed. He looked back at it and cracked up himself.

"What's in the other package?" my mother asked.

I opened it and held up a matching sweatshirt in my size. I held it up to me to show it off and said, "They were supposed to have our names on the other's shirt, but the printer made a mistake," I said.

I was pretty mad when they were delivered without names on them, but, we were all about the signs.

Mom told us she wanted a picture of us in our shirts and wanted us to put them on. He slid his over his head while I put mine on in my room. I said it was because I wanted to fix my hair, but I needed a few second alone to compose myself. Part of me wanted to argue with Mom and tell her this was not a moment I wanted to remember, but the other part reasoned that this would be the only picture I would ever have of him.

We stood in front of the door and Mom looked through the lens.

"Wait a minute," he said, and purposefully, ceremoniously took my hand. "Ready."

She snapped two pictures, then said thanks. "Well, it was nice knowing you," she said as she put her camera away.

"It's not like you'll never see me again," he said, looking from her to me.

"Don't say it if you don't mean it," Mom

said.

"I agree," I said, looking to him for confirmation.

"I'll be back up here. You wait and see," he said, reaching for the door.

I walked him out into the garage. "There's another volleyball game next weekend," I joked.

"I don't think I could make it up here that soon," he laughed back.

He had turned around to answer me, and with me on the step above him, we were on eye level. I took his face in my hands like he had done so many times to be and said, "I understand."

He made a total reformation from unhappy to relieved. He squeezed me tight. I had written him in one letter that I had needed a hug so I couldn't breathe for a week. He had written back that he was just the guy to do it!

He was holding me for the last time. He gave me one final squeeze and breathed, "Thank you."

It was such a simple way to say it, but I heard the emotion behind his words and began to cry again.

He tilted my head up and brushed away a tear. He was looking at me so intensely tenderly I felt somewhat self-conscious.

"What?" I asked.

"I'm just memorizing you. Your face, that smile, those eyes. I'm *really* going to miss you." He was so sincere, and somewhat surprised at himself. Was he just now realizing exactly how much he was going to miss me, now that the final moment was here? "Remember your promise about the book. I want to see your name in print."

"I will," I said. "I'm going to miss you, too."

He took my hand and placed it on his chest, over his heart. "You'll always be right here," he whispered. "I will always, always love you."

"And I will always love you," I whispered back, tears forming in my eyes again.

He pulled me back into his arms for one, last, bittersweet kiss.

Then he was gone.

Epilogue

I have only one piece of advice to my readers: *Always* buy boardwalk!